He found Krista cradling the baby against her chest

"How are you, sweetie?" she crooned, pressing a kiss on top of Joy's soft head. "I feel as if I neglected you today."

Hovering in the doorway, he watched as she sat in the rocker and held the baby on her knees, so Joy was facing her. He'd noticed Joy was very animated now that she was feeling better, making funny facial expressions while she waved her arms in uncoordinated movements.

"Aren't you just the cutest thing?" Krista said, smiling at the baby.

He stepped farther into the room. "Her auditory test results have confirmed a pretty significant hearing loss—in the eighty-five to ninety percent range—so she can't hear you."

Krista's startled glance met his. "I know."

He advanced into the room, unable to tear his gaze from the beautiful picture they made together.

Dear Reader,

Many of you met Abby Monroe in
The Consultant's Homecoming, and her brother
Alec Monroe in *Bride for a Single Dad.* I've had lots
of fun writing about the Monroe family, and since
many of you have been asking about the other
siblings, I've decided to continue writing the series.
Baby: Found at Christmas is Adam Monroe's story.

Christmas and children seem to go together.
Adam is a pediatrician and Krista is a pediatric
nurse at Children's Memorial Hospital. Krista has
always seen Adam as her hero, even when he was
engaged to her sister. Though that engagement
ended, he still sees Krista as a younger sister, not
as a desirable woman in her own right. But when
a small, abandoned baby brings them together,
they decide to join forces to find the identity of the
baby's mother. In the true spirit of Christmas and
forgiveness, Krista and Adam also find love.

I hope you enjoy Adam and Krista's story.

Happy reading!

Laura Iding

BABY: FOUND AT CHRISTMAS
Laura Iding

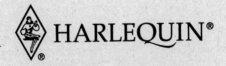

HARLEQUIN®

TORONTO • NEW YORK • LONDON
AMSTERDAM • PARIS • SYDNEY • HAMBURG
STOCKHOLM • ATHENS • TOKYO • MILAN • MADRID
PRAGUE • WARSAW • BUDAPEST • AUCKLAND

ISBN-13: 978-0-373-06630-8
ISBN-10:   0-373-06630-9

BABY: FOUND AT CHRISTMAS

First North American Publication 2007

www.eHarlequin.com

Printed in U.S.A.

BABY: FOUND AT CHRISTMAS

To Muna Shehadi Sill,
a fellow author and wonderful friend

CHAPTER ONE

ADAM MONROE rolled his shoulders and bent his head from side to side, working the crick out of his neck, trying to hide the depth of his exhaustion. "Doris, how many more patients are still waiting to be seen?"

"Just one more, in exam room number two." Doris, the receptionist, glanced at him with a frown. "You didn't eat lunch, did you?"

"No." Adam munched a stale cracker as he picked up the last patient's chart. They'd been extremely busy all day and well into the evening, but he knew the true source of his fatigue was plain, ordinary lack of sleep. Ever since the Christmas season had hit, the nightmares of the accident had returned. He shook off the feeling and glanced at Doris's concerned face. "Don't worry, I'll make up for it at dinner."

"Maybe teaming up with the public health department to offer medical care to low-income families wasn't such a good idea," Doris said in a low tone. "You're exhausted."

"Nonsense." As one of the founding partners of the private practice pediatric clinic, he was proud of their success. Tuesday evenings were reserved for the

public health department referrals. The first appoint-
ment was free, and if the patients needed more exten-
sive care and follow-up, subsequent visits were
pro-rated. "We're providing a great service. And,
besides, you know normally I'd have Phoebe's help
with this."

"True." Doris sighed. "I'll be glad when she's back
from her second honeymoon."

Phoebe Carmichael was his nurse practitioner, who
usually shared his patient load, especially the infants.
As she was currently off in the Caribbean, celebrating
her tenth wedding anniversary, he was on his own.

His stomach growled as he walked down the hall,
reading over the chart as he went. The patient was a
two-month-old baby and he mentally prepared
himself as he knocked briefly on the door before
walking in.

"Good evening, Ms Turner," he greeted the young
mother, who paced the room while holding a crying
baby against her shoulder. "I'm Dr Monroe. I understand Grady has been very fussy and has been running
a low-grade fever for the past twenty-four hours?"

"Yes." Grady's young mother appeared extremely
frazzled, as she bobbed the baby up and down, patting
the infant's back. The distress in her expression made
him fear she might actually start sobbing herself. "He
cries constantly. I try feeding him, changing him,
holding him—everything! Nothing works. There's
something seriously wrong with him, I just know it."

"I'll take a look," Adam promised. "Excessive crying
is very frustrating and could be from something simple
like an ear infection or colic." He maintained a profes-

sional demeanor, washing his hands in the sink and flashing Grady's mother a reassuring smile. He wished Phoebe was here to take this case.

"Would you, please, set him down on the table for a moment so I can examine him?" When she did so, he performed a thorough assessment. He tried to remain objective. When dealing with small infants, the history from the caregiver and the physical exam were the most important keys to a proper diagnosis.

Grady's temperature was normal, his eyes and ears were clear, no signs of infection. His heart and lungs sounded good, but his abdomen was tense with hyperactive bowel sounds. He asked about the baby's eating habits and bowel movements, and discovered Grady's mother was using a dairy-based formula.

He handed the child back with a sense of relief. "He's not running a fever at all now. I believe Grady has colic. He may have intolerance to milk, so I'd like you to try some soya-based formula for two weeks. I'll give you some samples, so you don't have to buy any unless it helps." He washed his hands again, while Ms Turner dressed the baby in his navy blue sleeper. "If that doesn't work, bring him back here and we can try something else. You were right to come in to see me. Babies shouldn't cry all the time."

"Thank you, Dr Monroe." Her eyes filled with gratitude.

"I'll give you an informational brochure on colic. There are some other tricks you can try, like using a baby swing or, as silly as it sounds, placing the car seat on top of your dryer while doing laundry. The motion seems to help settle a baby's upset stomach." He stood, holding Grady's chart. "I'll have Doris give you the formula samples, all right?"

"Yes." Grady's mother was already bundling him into his car carrier. "Thanks again for everything."

"You're welcome. Have a good evening." Adam left the exam room, walked past Doris, where she was seated at the front desk, and asked her to take the soya formula to Grady's mother.

He stared at the package of stale crackers, fighting a wave of desolation. As a pediatrician, he knew he couldn't avoid taking care of babies. Heck, they were the mainstay of his practice. He closed his eyes and rubbed his temple. How long would the past haunt him? To be fair, it had only been a year, but the Christmas reminders surrounding him didn't help. The memories of the past just wouldn't stay buried.

Somehow he needed to find the strength to get through this Christmas holiday. At least he was lucky to have a warm, loving, generous family to distract him from his guilt.

Time to finish up his paperwork and get out of here. He stacked the charts to one side, going through them to make sure his notes were clear and concise. Once he'd made sure everything was in order, Doris would need to send a copy of each record to the public health department.

His stomach grumbled again and, while he wasn't in the mood, he knew he needed to eat. Fast food didn't appeal, but it was quick and easy, and would stop the gnawing in his belly.

Maybe. Unless he had an ulcer.

"Adam!" Doris called out from the reception desk. "Come here, quick. Someone left a *baby*!"

"What?" Adam levered himself out of his seat, heading straight for the waiting area, thinking Doris had to be mistaken. "Are you sure?"

"Look!" Doris waved a hand at the empty waiting room. "I know that baby wasn't there thirty minutes ago."

He stared, not sure if his glucose-deprived brain was playing tricks on him. He blinked. Nope, still there. A small, crying baby, safely tucked in an infant car seat which had been left on one of the waiting room chairs.

"I'll check the bathrooms," Doris said over her shoulder as she headed down the hall to the public rest-rooms their office shared with the adult walk-in clinic down the hall.

Adam moved closer. The baby was dressed from head to toe in a bright pink sleeper. Unless the color was some sort of a bizarre joke, he assumed the baby was a girl. He gauged her to be six weeks old, her tiny face scrunched and red from crying.

A folded slip of paper was tucked between the baby and the car-seat cushion. Fearing the worst, he pulled it out and read the words, carefully printed. "I'm sorry but I can't take care of Joy any more. Please find her a good home. I brought her here because she's been running a fever for the past two days."

Abandoned? Someone had actually abandoned a small infant in his waiting room?

"There's no sign of a parent anywhere—I even checked the men's room!" Doris huffed in an attempt to catch her breath.

Adam handed her the note. "You're sure you didn't see anyone drop her off?"

"No. You know how busy we were. After putting the

last patient into an exam room, I spent the rest of the time trying to get caught up on filing. I didn't see or hear anyone come in." Doris's eyes widened when she read the note in his hand. "I can't believe this! Who would abandon their baby like this? Especially three weeks before Christmas?"

The baby's crying, which didn't quite sound right, grated on his nerves. He had a new appreciation for why Grady's mother had appeared so frazzled. "Pick her up, will you? I'll have to examine her."

"Sure." Doris was already working the buckle on the car seat. The minute Doris lifted the baby against her shoulder, Joy quietened down. "Oh, my, she really is warm."

Adam grabbed the car seat. He was concerned about the baby's fever. "Take her into the first exam room."

Doris carefully set the baby girl on the exam table. "Do you think she's hungry?"

"Yeah. Go ahead and make a bottle from the samples of formula. We don't know when she was last fed. Could be the mother ran out of money for milk." Thank heavens he always carried a sizable stockpile of extra supplies in case of emergencies.

Like this.

Doris hustled off, leaving him to carefully remove the bright pink sleeper. Doris was right—the baby radiated heat from her tiny body. When he checked her temperature, he wasn't surprised to discover her fever was high, 39.4° C.

Joy's cry had a barking sound to it. He listened to her lungs, not surprised to hear diminished breath sounds. Could the baby have RSV—respiratory syncytial virus? He needed to do more tests, cultures and maybe an X-ray of her chest. This baby needed more care than he could provide here, in his clinic.

Even taking baby Joy to the hospital, though, wouldn't necessarily help him provide a firm diagnosis. Not when he didn't have a caregiver to give him a complete history. How well was she eating? How long had she had this barking cry? How many hours did she sleep at a time? Too many questions without any answers.

"Here's the bottle," Doris said, entering the room. "I hope she'll take it."

He hoped so, too. There was no way of knowing if Joy's mother had breast-fed her, bottle-fed her or used a special soya-based formula. All he could do is hope for the best through trial and error.

Once he'd finished his exam, he bundled Joy back into her pink sleeper, fumbling a bit with the snaps. He intended to hand the baby straight over to Doris, she was more of an expert in this area than he was, but the moment he lifted Joy against his chest, she quieted down.

Awestruck, he stared down at her for a long moment. She was beautiful, her dainty features perfect. Tearing his gaze from her tiny face, he forced himself to think like a doctor. Joy's weight was on the low side for around six weeks old, and he wondered if the mother truly couldn't afford to feed the child. Breast-milk was free but, still, if money was an issue, he'd much rather have the baby here than anywhere else.

"Do you want me to try and feed her?" Betty asked, still holding the bottle.

"Yes, please." Strangely reluctant, he handed the

baby over, knowing he should use the time to finish writing up his assessment. But he found it difficult to concentrate, too intent on watching to see if Joy took the formula or not.

The baby latched onto the nipple for a few minutes, sucking eagerly. But she didn't take nearly as much nourishment as he would have liked. Too soon she let go and turned her face away.

"Now what?" Doris wrinkled her forehead in concern.

As much as he didn't want this baby to be his problem, he knew he couldn't ignore her illness. "I'll take her to Children's Memorial Hospital as a direct admission." Adam gathered the few sheets of paper together—so far, his notes were all that Joy had as far as a medical record was concerned. "Her fever needs attention."

He couldn't do a complete work-up here, his clinic wasn't equipped with a full lab. Joy's ears had looked clear, but he wanted blood and spinal-fluid cultures. "Put the baby back into the car seat."

As Doris buckled Joy in, he grabbed his coat. Winter in Milwaukee, Wisconsin, was cold. He searched through his cabinets to get an old blanket, tossing it over the baby to protect her face from the frigid temperatures.

She began to cry again, the sound only partially muffled by the blanket. He forced himself to ignore the pathetic sound as he hefted the infant seat in one hand and headed for the door.

"Wait—don't you think we should call the police?" Doris appeared crestfallen at not being able to follow him all the way to the hospital. It was on the tip of his tongue to ask her to come with him, which was ridiculous, as there was really nothing Doris could do.

"Not a bad idea." He glanced at his watch, unable to ignore the sense of urgency. "My brother Alec is a cop, a detective for the Milwaukee PD. I'll call him on the way. Go home, Doris. Thanks for your help. Drive safe," he added as he stepped into the bitter cold.

The *Farmer's Almanac* had claimed this would be one of their colder winters yet, and so far he was forced to agree. The wind felt like it was twenty below zero as it tore against his face. He ducked his head to avoid it. At least it wasn't snowing, but his feet crunched on snow and ice as he carefully made his way to his car.

With new respect for mothers who lugged their babies around on a regular basis, he secured the infant car seat in the back seat. He swore under his breath when he couldn't figure out how to get the carrier buckled into the car. Eventually he understood he needed to weave the seat belt behind the straps before latching it, a task easier said than done. After closing the back door, he quickly slid behind the wheel. His office wasn't far from Children's Memorial Hospital and he let the car run for a few minutes to warm up the engine.

Joy's cries echoed throughout the interior of the car. He gripped the steering-wheel, unable to do anything to stop her crying. He hadn't felt this helpless since the accident last year. His son would have been almost six months old if he'd lived. "Hang in there, Joy, we're almost there." Adam glanced at the car seat in his rear-view mirror but couldn't see the baby's face. He continued to talk to her, hoping the sound of his voice would help let her know she wasn't alone.

His attempts to calm her were in vain. She was still

crying when he eased into traffic, using his hands-off phone to call Alec.

"Hey, Alec," Adam greeted his brother when he answered the phone. "I have a little problem."

"What's up?" Alec paused, and then added, "Is that a baby?"

"Yeah. That's my problem." Adam sighed. "She was abandoned in my clinic. I'm taking her to Children's Memorial. Would you meet me there?"

"Sure." Alec didn't hesitate. "May take some time. I need to arrange for someone to watch Shelby. Jillian's at work."

A flash of guilt nagged at him. He hated dragging his brother away from his family. Alec and Jillian had only been married for a month and were still trying to make their respective schedules mesh. "Don't rush. You can wait until Jillian gets home. Thanks, Alec."

He disconnected the line and pulled into the parking lot of Children's Memorial Hospital.

"We're here, Joy." Unbuckling the car seat was almost as complicated as getting it together. "Don't cry, everything is going to be fine."

Adam was glad he could admit the baby to the hospital where he could keep an eye on her. Once Alec arrived, it would only be a matter of time before Social Services got involved. There had to be a way to track down the baby's mother. There were ways of getting financial support, and he could help Joy's mother navigate the system. The public health department had a variety of programs, as did Children's Memorial Hospital. Maybe Joy's mother didn't realize the resources that were available.

He wanted to see Joy reunited with her mother. Although his first priority was to discover the source of Joy's fever.

"Admitting just called with a new patient. This one is yours, Krista."

"No problem." Krista glanced up from the chart she was reviewing. Emily, charge nurse for Six South, had taken the last admission, so indeed this new patient was hers. She didn't mind. She liked this unit, where the patients were infants up to the age of about two years, especially because she learned something new every day. "Where is the admission coming from? The ED?"

"Nope, Dr Monroe is bringing this one over as a direct admission. The patient is a six-week-old baby with a fever of unknown origin. Put her in Bed 618, as it's directly across from the nurses' station."

Krista momentarily froze. Dr Monroe? As in Dr Adam Monroe?

"Krista?" She glanced up to see Emily frowning at her. "Is something wrong?"

"No, of course not," she lied. Closing the chart she stood. "I'll go set up the room."

Ducking into the empty patient room, Krista leaned up against the wall, trying to calm her racing heart. Over the past six months, since she'd started this job, she'd never had to take any of Adam's patients. She'd seen him on the unit now and then, but so far he hadn't recognized her, simply nodding or saying hello before going on his way.

She'd known this day would come, but felt woefully

unprepared for it now. Talking to him, after nearly a year, would feel awkward.

Why on earth was he bringing a direct admission in himself? If the baby was that sick, wouldn't he admit directly to the PICU? Maybe he wouldn't stay long, simply drop the patient off and then leave.

She pushed away from the wall and went to the supply room to fetch an LP tray, knowing that babies with fevers usually needed a lumbar puncture procedure. When she returned, she set the equipment near the small procedure table. She sighed, forced to admit that dropping the baby off wouldn't be Adam Monroe's usual style. He had a reputation for being extremely thorough. Everyone liked him. Nurses had been known to vie for his attention.

She couldn't blame them—if circumstances had been different she might have vied for his attention, too.

After making sure there were enough sterile drapes in the drawer of the procedure table, she stepped back and ran her fingers through her short blonde-streaked curls. There was no reason to worry. If Adam Monroe hadn't recognized her by now, he wasn't likely to recognize her at all. She'd cut her limp brown hair to allow her natural wave to come through and had added highlights. She'd also had laser surgery for her near-sightedness, as her eyes hadn't been able to get used to contact lenses. The laser surgery had been something of a necessity. On the second day of her orientation, an eight-month-old boy had grabbed her glasses and tossed them onto the floor, forcing her to wear the broken glasses for the remainder of her shift.

Regardless of why she'd altered her appearance,

Krista knew she looked completely different, compared to a year and a half ago, when she'd first met Adam. He had dated her older sister Danielle, the two of them becoming engaged after six months. She hadn't seen him since last Christmas, after Danielle had broken off their engagement and moved overseas.

She'd only spoken with him a couple of times, having been away at college for much of the time he and Danielle had dated. Did he even remember she'd been enrolled in a nursing program? One of her most vivid memories was of the night he'd come over to pick up Danielle while her Aunt Bea had been there. Krista had been concerned when the woman had lost her balance, twice. She'd asked Adam to take a look and between them they'd examined Bea, quickly coming to the conclusion she had been having a minor stroke.

The moments they'd worked together had proved she'd made the right choice in becoming a nurse. She'd always been drawn to helping people, especially kids, and talking to Adam had only reinforced how attending college to major in nursing had been the right thing to do.

Krista crossed over to smooth the sheet over the crib mattress. She pulled out an extra blanket and set it at the foot of the crib. Glancing around, she noted everything was ready. There wasn't much more for her to do.

Except continue to stand there, anticipating Adam's arrival. Hiding in her patient's room. How pathetic. Hadn't she changed at all over the past eighteen months? More than her outward appearance, she'd been striving to become more self-confident, more outgoing and assertive.

Enough time had passed for her to get over her secret crush on Adam Monroe.

Danielle wouldn't have hidden in an empty patient room. Her older sister had always reacted a little differently to things than she had. When they'd been shuffled from one relative's house to the other, Danielle had only gotten into more trouble, while Krista had become quieter and well behaved. She loved her sister, had really missed her since Danielle had temporarily moved to London.

"Which room?" she heard a deep male voice ask.

"Right behind you, Dr Monroe, in 618." Emily's voice was clear. "I think Krista is in there, getting things ready."

"Thanks."

She barely had time to turn around before he walked in.

For a moment their gazes locked, his green eyes mesmerizing, holding her captive. She almost took a step back from the impact. Instead, she forced herself to stand her ground.

"Krista? Krista Vaughn?" He stared at her, recognition dawning in his eyes. "How long have you worked here?"

CHAPTER TWO

"I, UM, about six months." Adam had recognized her. She couldn't believe he'd recognized her. A secret thrill warred with disappointment. Obviously she didn't look as different as she'd hoped. She cleared her throat, willing herself not to say something stupid, and stepped aside to give him access to the crib. The sleeve of his leather coat brushed against her arm as he set the infant car seat on the mattress. His musky male scent, intermixed with leather, clouded her senses.

Bringing back memories she found impossible to ignore.

Focus on the patient, she told herself sternly. He stepped away just as she moved forward and they bumped into each other. His hand came up to grasp her arm, steadying her. She hoped her reaction to his touch wasn't too noticeable as she said, "The baby is adorable. What's her name?"

"Joy Smith, for lack of anything better." Adam let go of her and took a step back. She could still feel the warm imprint from his grasp on her arm. Her cheeks burned as she quickly busied herself with the baby.

Then his words registered. "For lack of anything

better?" she repeated, frowning as she unbuckled the straps of the car seat. "Don't you know her name?"

"Her first name is Joy, but I don't know her last name." Adam tunneled his hand through his sable-colored hair, leaving it mussed. "We found her in my waiting room."

"You're kidding." Her initial discomfort faded. Adam had recognized her but hadn't mentioned or asked after Danielle, which confused her. Had he gotten over her sister or not? She sincerely hoped he had as she happened to know Danielle was dating someone else. Her gaze dropped back down to the crying infant. "Abandoned? Poor thing." She lifted the baby out of the seat and laid her on the crib mattress. "She feels hot."

"Last rectal temp was 39.4° C. I need you to get an IV in her and then draw blood to send cultures. Once all that is finished, we'll need to do a lumbar puncture."

She picked up the baby, who immediately quieted against her. "I'll call down to the ED, let them know we'll need a resident to come up and do the LP."

Adam frowned, shaking his head. "No need. I'll do the procedure."

"You?" Krista couldn't hide her surprise. After all, the hour was late, almost nine o'clock at night. There had to be other things Adam would rather do on a Tuesday evening. Danielle had broken off their engagement after the accident. Surely he'd begun to date again in the year that had passed.

"Yes, me." He raised a brow at her incredulous tone. "I'll write a series of admission orders while you get started."

"Of course." When Adam left, she stared at the

empty doorway for a moment, remembering the time he'd rescued her from a second date gone bad. She'd called Danielle to come and pick her up, but Adam had answered the phone instead because her sister hadn't been feeling well. He'd immediately come for her, angry at how her date had been a little too enthusiastic about getting his end-of-the-night kiss. She'd been a mess, emotionally more so than physically, and Adam had given her a hug, offering comfort.

She'd known he'd thought of her like a younger sister, but after that night her feelings for him had morphed into something more. Maybe because her track record with men hadn't been exactly great. She seemed to have a tendency to find losers, making it too easy to think of Adam as her knight in shining armor. Thank heavens her spring break from college had ended and she hadn't had to face Adam again for a long time afterwards.

Joy squirmed in her embrace, reminding her that she had work to do. She bent her head to nuzzle Joy's downy head with her cheek.

Abandoned. What a shame. And such a beautiful baby, too. Would the mother return? Possibly. Especially being so close to Christmas. In her mind, Christmas and babies were meant to go together.

Krista set the baby on the pull-out procedure table, removed the bright pink sleeper and strapped Joy securely so she wouldn't fall off. Starting IVs on babies was the hardest thing she'd had to learn during her transition from nursing adults to nursing children.

She'd managed to place the IV on the first stick and was basking in the glow of her success when Adam returned.

"Have you drawn her blood yet?"

She sensed his impatience and flushed. "Yes, I drew blood off the IV site for the first sample. I only need one more culture from a different site."

"Good." He watched as she finished dressing the area. "Doris, my receptionist at the clinic, tried to feed her, but she didn't take much, not even a full ounce."

At six weeks the baby should have been taking at least two ounces of formula at a feeding. Krista hid her dismay. "I suppose we don't have any sort of history from the mother?"

"No." Adam's brow furrowed. "We may want to try a couple of different types of formula on her."

She nodded in agreement. "Do you want me to draw the second blood sample or would you rather do the lumbar puncture first?"

"Go ahead and draw the second lot of blood culture."

Self-conscious as he was watching her, she wished he'd leave. But he didn't. Ignoring him wasn't easy, although luck was on her side when she found another scalp vein and managed to draw the blood without difficulty.

"Will you watch her for a minute so I can send these off to the lab?" she asked, raising her voice over the sounds of Joy's crying.

There was a moment's hesitation before Adam nodded and stepped toward the procedure table. "Sure."

Skirting around him, she grabbed the first tiny tube of blood and headed to the main nursing station. At Children's Memorial, runners hand-delivered all blood to the lab, the precious samples not being entrusted to the pneumatic tube system. Once she'd labeled them and handed them to the runner, she returned to Joy's room.

And halted abruptly in the doorway, when she saw Adam cradling the infant against his broad chest.

Her heart thudded, her throat squeezing shut.

What was it about a strong man holding a baby that turned a woman to mush? Here she'd thought the stupid crush she'd harbored for her sister's former fiancé was dead but, no, suddenly, frighteningly the old feelings had flared back to life.

Somehow, she had to find the strength to stay away from Adam, so he'd never discover how she really felt.

Adam did his best to ignore his odd reaction to Krista. The flash of physical awareness had taken him by surprise. Not because he harbored any lingering feelings toward her sister Danielle but more because he'd always considered Krista as if she were his kid sister. After all, she was closer to Abby's age.

It was disconcerting to realize the sweet kid had grown into a beautiful woman.

Krista carefully held Joy in position as he slid the spinal needle between the tiny baby's first and second lumbar vertebrae. How strange after all these months to run into Krista again, especially here, working at Children's Memorial Hospital.

Focus on the procedure, he reminded himself. When a drop of cerebrospinal fluid appeared at the end of the lumen, he stopped advancing the needle. "Hand me the first tube, would you?" he asked over the baby's crying.

Krista handed over the small plastic specimen container. Holding the needle steady, he let several drops of cerebral spinal fluid fall into the receptacle before closing the cap and asking for the next one. Once all the tubes were filled, he used a sterile two by two and withdrew the needle.

Normally he didn't have trouble blocking women from his mind, especially when working, but Krista smelled like Christmas, a subtle mix of evergreen trees and cranberries, and the tantalizing scent distracted him.

She was cute with her hair cut short, curling softly around her face. Danielle had been tall, beautiful in a glamorous sort of way. Krista didn't physically resemble her sister much, but the moment he'd looked down into her wide brown eyes he'd recognized her.

He snuck another glance at her, but she was trying to soothe the crying infant. He must have passed her around the hospital but, if so, he hadn't made the connection. For sure they'd never shared a patient.

Until now.

Joy's cries were getting weaker. If anything, the IV fluids should be helping to rehydrate her.

"Did you order antibiotics?" Krista asked, reading his mind.

"Yes." He watched as she quickly stripped away the sterile field. "Now that we have both sets of samples drawn, I'd like her to get the first dose ASAP."

"Of course." Krista reached to unstrap the baby from the procedure table just as he did.

What was he doing? Baby Joy was his patient, nothing more. In fact, he almost wished Joy's mother had chosen some other clinic to abandon her baby in.

No, that wasn't true. He sighed. He hadn't consciously avoided infants over this past year since he and Danielle had lost their child, but it had certainly helped to know Phoebe had preferred taking care of the younger ones.

And if Phoebe had been here, he might not have gotten to know Joy. Or Krista.

"I'll take care of her," Krista informed him. She dressed the baby and set her safely in the crib. She pulled up the bar so Joy wouldn't fall out. "I'll see if Pharmacy has sent the medication yet."

He nodded, unable to tear his gaze from the baby, grimacing at his foolishness. The accident had been his fault. His stubbornness had cost his son's life. Holding Joy was a painful reminder of what he'd lost. Reuniting the baby with her mother wasn't going to atone for his sins.

Nothing would turn back the clock, no matter how much he wished he could.

His stomach clenched, and a familiar nausea haunted him as he relived those painful moments. The screeching tires, the horrible crash of metal against metal as the semi-trailer had barreled into them. He'd swerved, trying to avoid the contact, but seconds too late. The passenger side, where Danielle had been sitting, had been hit with enough force to deploy the airbags.

Danielle had survived with surprisingly few injuries, but the seat belt across her lap had left bruises. Considering she'd only been five and a half months pregnant, the doctor had prepared them for the eventual miscarriage.

Their relationship hadn't survived the tragedy. No surprise, when their rocky relationship had contributed to the tragedy.

"Pharmacy has sent the antibiotic dose." Krista returned, triumphantly holding a small syringe he assumed was the medication.

"Great." He stared down at Joy, realizing there was no longer any reason for him to stay. Except to wait for Alec. With a frown he glanced at his watch. He'd hoped his brother would be there by now.

Krista diluted the antibiotic in the burritrol chamber of the IV and set the appropriate rate on the pump before giving him a puzzled glance. "Ah—is there anything else, Adam? I have things under control if you need to get going."

Leaving the infant in Krista's capable hands would be the sensible thing to do, but as he had to wait for Alec, there was no reason for them both to stay. Krista no doubt had other patients to tend to. "I don't know if you remember my brother Alec, he's a Milwaukee detective and he's supposed to meet me here. I can watch her if you have other patients to see."

"All right." She hesitated in the doorway, glancing back at him. "What will happen to her?"

He lifted a shoulder. "I imagine once she's medically cleared, she'll go into foster-care until someone can adopt her. Unless her mother returns in time." And if he had his way, he'd find the mother to give the woman a chance to change her mind.

Krista frowned, as if she'd expected his answer. "So she'll end up in foster-care."

Not if he could find the mother. A poignant silence fell and Adam realized he and Krista were completely in tune over the fate of this precious little girl. Neither one of them wanted to see her go into foster-care, even though the baby's young age practically guaranteed a quick adoption.

The idea of a nice family taking Joy into their hearts should have reassured him. But it didn't. He couldn't shake the sense that Joy belonged with her mother.

"I'll leave you alone, then," Krista murmured, as she backed toward the door. "Call me if you need anything."

"I will."

She flashed a quick smile before disappearing through the doorway. Her smile stayed with him for a long time. For some reason he remembered the night he'd driven out to pick her up from a date who'd gotten too enthusiastic with his attentions. He'd been so angry on her behalf it had taken every ounce of self-control he'd possessed not to plant his fist in the guy's face.

Krista had deserved better.

Alec walked into the room, interrupting his thoughts. "Hey, Alec," he greeted his brother. "Thanks for coming."

"No problem." His brother drew out a small note-book. "Now tell me exactly what happened?"

"What do you mean? Baby found in waiting room with a note. What else is there?"

Alec gave an exasperated snort. "Details. I need details."

"I don't have any details." Adam handed over the note. "Other than this."

Alec took the note, examining it closely. "Where was it?"

"Tucked in the side of the infant carrier, like this." Adam demonstrated.

"Hmm. Seems like this was a well thought-out abandonment," Alec mused, glancing at Adam. "Not likely a teen mother."

His own thought exactly. "I'd like to find her. Joy's mother, I mean."

His brother stared at him. "We don't have much to go on."

"Yeah, I get that, but I still want to try. Will you help me?"

Alec shrugged. "Sure. But be prepared to be disappointed. We probably won't find her unless she's changed her mind and returns on her own."

"I know." He was glad Alec had agreed to help. His unborn son hadn't stood a chance, the odds had been stacked against him even before the truck had hit them.

Things would work out better for Joy. He'd search for the mother every spare second he had if necessary.

Krista stared at Joy with a troubled frown. The baby was getting worse instead of better. Joy's respiratory rate and pulse had increased significantly, despite the breathing treatments and antibiotics Adam had ordered.

She bit her lip and inwardly debated her next step. Normally, in this instance, she'd call the mother—if the patient's parents weren't already at the bedside—and then the doctor. But in this case the only person other than herself who really cared about Joy's condition was Adam Monroe.

How did he feel about being called at home? Eleven o'clock at night wasn't horribly late, but he'd only been gone a little less than two hours. For all she knew, he'd be irritated with her for waking him up, if he had already gone to bed.

Don't go there. She squeezed her eyes shut as if to escape the vision. Imagining Adam, warm and tousled in bed, was *not* helping.

She gazed back down at the sleeping infant tucked in the curve of her arm. Should she wait or should she call? What if the baby got worse? Wouldn't it be better to call Adam now, rather than delay the inevitable for another couple of hours when he would, no doubt, be deeply asleep?

She stared at Joy, trying to be objective when her feelings toward Adam were anything but. Telling herself she wasn't making excuses to call him only made her feel a little better. Joy was getting worse. And she'd extended her shift another four hours to cover a sick call, which made this phone call to Adam a necessity.

With a sigh she stood and made her way over to the phone. If Joy's condition grew worse, she'd have no choice but to call anyway to arrange a transfer to the PICU.

She didn't page him, unsure whether or not he kept his pager on when he wasn't on call. The hospital operator gave her Adam's home phone number and she wrote the number down on a slip of paper. Keeping the baby in the crook of her arm, she placed the call.

"Hello?"

Good heavens, his deep voice, husky with sleep, had made her knees go weak. This was exactly what she'd been afraid of.

She took a calming breath and told herself to stop being an idiot. "I'm sorry to bother you, Adam, but Joy is getting worse. Her respirations are up to 48 per

minute and her pulse is over 160." Krista bit her lip,
trying not to show the depth of her concern.. "She's
more lethargic, too. And she hasn't taken a full ounce
of formula."

"What's her pulse ox?" He sounded more awake
now. "And how do her lungs sound?"

"Her lungs sound the same, although we just
finished giving her a breathing treatment. Her pulse ox
is still hanging in the low nineties. I was thinking maybe
we should try a croup tent."

"Yeah, that's a good idea." There was a brief silence,
before Adam added, "I'll be right in."

"No!" The exclamation slipped out before she could
catch herself. "I mean," she hastily amended, "that
isn't necessary. I swear I've been keeping a close eye
on her. I won't take any chances. If her condition
doesn't improve, I'll have the ED resident arrange a
transfer to the PICU."

"I trust you, Krista, but it's after eleven. Isn't your
shift over?"

"No, I agreed to stay an additional four hours."

"Good." The relief in his tone warmed her heart. "I
feel better knowing you're there to watch over her. Her
lethargy worries me."

"I agree." The increase in Joy's vital signs could
mean the antibiotics were trying to fight off the infection, but the decreased pulse ox and lethargy were bad
signs. "Is there anything else we should do?"

"Try the croup tent. If that doesn't work, call me
back. She may need to be intubated."

Krista knew he was right, but she also knew that
babies who needed to be intubated at this young age

often suffered other adverse effects, like potential damage to their lungs. She hoped Joy's respiratory status improved so it wouldn't come to that. "I will."

"Thanks for calling."

Thank heavens he couldn't see the goofy smile on her face. "You're welcome."

Feeling better, she hung up the phone and then quickly made arrangements for a croup tent to be set up. For the croup tent to work, she'd need to set the baby down, which little Joy didn't seem to like much, but if it helped her breathing, using the tent was worth the effort.

Luckily, Krista's other tiny patients were doing fine, and all of them, except, of course, for Joy, had a parent spending the night with them. After the croup tent was set up and Joy safely nestled inside, she made the rounds of her other patients, feeling a tad guilty at how she longed to stay near Joy's side.

She tried to rationalize that Joy needed her more because there wasn't anyone else to stay with her, but she knew that wasn't the only reason. In the few hours she'd been assigned to take care of her, baby Joy had touched her heart.

All her life she'd longed for a family. Caring for Joy only reinforced her need to belong.

She assessed the baby again after Joy had spent thirty minutes in the croup tent. Joy's respiratory rate came down to 42 breaths per minute and her pulse ox was up to a whopping 94 per cent.

Progress, but not enough to consider Joy safely out of the danger zone.

A noise outside the door made her jump around in

surprise. Her elbow jerked, knocking the clipboard to the floor with a loud clatter. She immediately winced and glanced at Joy lying on her back in the tent, but the baby hadn't woken up.

"Sorry, didn't mean to scare you." Adam stepped into the room, stealing her breath in his well-worn pale blue jeans and a navy sweatshirt instead of his usual shirt, tie and white lab coat.

"I'm fine." At least she would be in a few minutes, once her heart got over its momentary lack of oxygen. As she glanced down at the clipboard, she frowned, re-alizing how strange it was that the clatter hadn't woken Joy up. Worried, she leaned over and touched the baby, feeling for a pulse.

Joy responded to her touch, her tiny fists waving in startled surprise when she woke up. Thankfully, the baby's lethargy didn't seem as bad as before.

"How is she?" Adam crossed the room to stand beside her, gazing down at the crib.

"Better, I think." She handed him the clipboard. "Her vitals seem to be responding to the croup tent."

"I'm pretty sure she has RSV, so I'm not surprised." Adam reviewed the information on the flow sheet, then set the clipboard aside and tucked his hands into the front pockets of his jeans. "If we can get her through the night, I'm sure she'll be better by tomorrow."

She nodded, shooting him a sidelong glance. "I thought you trusted me?"

The corner of his mouth crooked up in a half-smile. "I do. I tried to go back to sleep, but couldn't. Figured I was better off here, helping you."

Krista smiled, even though the last thing she needed was to spend the night in a patient's room in close contact with Adam.

She liked him far too much already.

CHAPTER THREE

AN AWKWARD silence fell as they both watched baby Joy sleep. Krista bit her lip and tried to think of something to say. It seemed as if they were both avoiding any mention of her sister. She wished more than anything she knew how he felt about the broken engagement.

"Krista?" Jenny, one of the night-shift nurses, called loudly into the room. "We're getting something to eat from the cafeteria. Did you want something?"

"Ah, no, I'm fine." She swung toward Adam, thankful for something inane to talk about. "Are you hungry?"

"No, thanks." He smiled and she found herself noticing the way his eyes crinkled at the corners.

Stop it, she admonished herself. This was ridiculous. He was just being nice, courteous as they took care of a very sick baby.

Her gaze dropped to the monitor where the baby's pulse-ox and heart-rate readings flashed on the screen. Joy had once again fallen asleep. Gazing at the baby, she couldn't shake the feeling that something wasn't right. After a few minutes, she put her finger on the problem.

Joy hadn't moved a bit when Jenny had called her name or when she'd dropped the clipboard. Thinking back through her shift, Krista realized Joy only responded to being touched or held.

Grabbing the clipboard from Adam's hands, she threw it loudly to the floor, without taking her eyes off Joy.

"What are you doing?" Adam exclaimed, jumping as the loud clatter reverberated through the room. "Trying to give me a heart attack?"

Krista swung around to face him, her eyes wide. "She didn't move, Adam. Not a single muscle. I think it's possible Joy is deaf."

Adam stared at Krista, wondering how she'd figured out something he, as the pediatrician, had missed. "Deaf," he repeated. "That would explain a lot. No wonder she always quieted down when someone held her. She couldn't hear voices to know someone was near."

"The poor thing," Krista murmured. "I wonder if her mother figured it out?" her gaze collided with his. "Do you think it's the reason she abandoned her?"

"No." Adam didn't want to think the worst. He knew there were some horrible parents, he'd seen a couple of child-abuse cases he'd reported over the past few years. But he hadn't seen any unexplained bruises or injuries when he'd examined Joy. The mother's note led him to believe she would have mentioned the deafness if she had known. Hadn't she clued him in to Joy's fever? "I'll order more testing so we can discover the extent of Joy's hearing loss. Maybe it's not as bad as we're thinking."

"Maybe," Krista agreed, but her tone held a note of doubt. "Guess all my talking and singing was for naught."

He had to laugh, remembering how he'd talked to Joy in the car. "Mine, too."

Krista's expression was troubled. "Adam, if the mother doesn't come back, her deafness could affect her likelihood of being adopted."

His smile faded. "Yeah, I know. She could qualify for a cochlear transplant, but they won't do the surgery until she's at least twelve months old." And even then he doubted Joy's mother could afford the expensive procedure. Even with financial help from government-based programs, there were potentially ongoing costs which might not be covered, anything from specialist care to simple battery replacements.

Krista tapped her fingers on the small CD player she'd set up, playing Christmas carols as soft background music. "I guess I could turn this off."

It was on the tip of his tongue to agree—he didn't need more reminders of Christmas. But her wistful expression confirmed his suspicion that Krista had put the music on as much for herself as for Joy. He knew what her and Danielle's lives had been like after they'd lost their parents. Danielle had told him how they'd ended up being shuffled from one relative to another. No one had wanted them on a permanent basis.

"Leave it on." He could manage to put up with the Christmas tunes, for her sake.

A shy smile tugged the corner of her mouth. "All right."

Staring at Krista, he suddenly realized he'd come in tonight for more than just to double-check on Joy.

Despite his desire to forget about the past, he'd come to see Krista.

The next morning, Krista overslept. So much for her plan to get some Christmas shopping done. After taking a quick shower, she pulled on a clean set of scrubs with a bright colorful Christmas-tree pattern and had just enough time to grab something to eat before she needed to leave.

Staring at her bowl of cereal, she wondered how Joy had fared through the rest of her night. Adam had left about the same time she had, at two in the morning, insisting on walking her out to her car.

Of course, he hadn't kissed her goodnight or anything but for a moment there when he'd gazed intently down at her, she'd thought he might.

Unless the fleeting thought had been nothing more than her overactive imagination. She sighed. She really needed to get over her feelings for Adam. Especially as she didn't know how he felt about her sister. There had to be a non-threatening, casual way to mention Danielle. She simply couldn't stand the thought of Adam pining away for Danielle for a whole year. Danielle hadn't said much about her break-up with Adam, except to mention how they were fighting a lot and didn't have the same goals for their future.

And if that had truly been the case, Adam couldn't still be in love with Danielle.

Could he?

Had Danielle ever mentioned *her* crush to Adam? Heavens, she hoped not. She grimaced. How embarrassing.

Danielle had been shaken up after their car accident. Krista had been away at school when it had happened and as far as she knew, Danielle had only spent one night in the hospital for observation. By the time Krista had discovered what had happened and rushed back to

Milwaukee, Danielle had already been discharged home. She'd made arrangements to move to London within the week.

And Krista had never spoken to Adam again. Until now.

Enough brooding over the man. Even if Adam was over Danielle, he no doubt still thought of Krista as a younger sister. Now that she'd cut her hair, lost a few pounds and had had laser surgery on her eyes, men did tend to notice her. Still, it wasn't as if she had dozens of men lining up to ask her out. She'd watched women flirt and often wondered why she couldn't seem to master the art.

Maybe it was all Adam's fault. She couldn't send out those, *I'm interested* vibes because she'd always measured other men against Adam, finding the others seriously lacking.

Giving up on her breakfast, she rinsed her dishes and grabbed her purse. She'd spent so much time thinking about Adam she had less than fifteen minutes to get to work.

She practically ran down the hall of her apartment building, not wanting to be late. The tedious job of scraping ice off her windshield while the frigid wind blew against her face cost her a few additional minutes.

As she walked onto Six South with a minute to spare, she noticed a bustle of activity halfway down the hall, a few feet away from the nurses' station.

Not Joy's room, thank heavens, but Krista hurried over to see if her peers needed help.

"What's going on?" she asked, entering the room. Two nurses stood over a baby lying in a crib.

"Devon has been vomiting for the past hour," Wendy said, a small frown in her brow. "Come here, Krista, do you smell something funny?"

Krista stepped forward and nodded. "Yeah, something sweet. You'd better call Devon's doctor. The baby needs to be tested for ketoacidosis."

"That's what I thought," Wendy admitted. "Would you do me a favor and call Dr Monroe? I don't want to leave the baby alone and his mother went home for a little while."

"Sure." Krista hurried back out to the nurses' station and asked for Adam Monroe to be paged. He returned the call in less than a minute.

"This is Adam Monroe. I was paged?"

"Yes, this is Krista on Six South. Wendy asked me to let you know Devon Gibson, the baby in room 612, has been vomiting for the past hour. His breath smells sickly sweet and we think he needs to be tested for DKA."

"Absolutely," Adam agreed without hesitation. "Draw a basic chemistry panel and call me as soon as you have the results."

"I will." Krista wrote down the order. "Anything else?"

"Not at the moment." There was a slight pause before he added, "Krista? Keep a close eye on him. If Devon really has DKA as a one-month-old, then he has a very serious underlying illness."

She'd heard of cases where young infants had severe acidosis to the point where they arrested and died. But she'd never taken care of one herself. "Maybe we should transfer him to the PICU."

"I'm in clinic and only have one more patient to see.

As soon as I'm finished here, I'll head over. Draw the blood samples and we'll take it from there."

He was right, there was no need to panic yet. But she was still very nervous as she hung up the phone. With a hurried step she went back into Devon's room to help Wendy.

By the time she'd gotten Devon's blood drawn, the baby had become her patient by default. The rest of the second shift nurses had made out the patient assignments, giving her only two babies for now, Joy and Devon, leaving her open for the first admission.

Both were Adam's patients. What were the odds? For six months she hadn't taken care of any of his patients— now she had the only two patients of his on the entire floor.

Thank heavens Joy was doing fairly well at the moment. Krista knew Devon would need most of her attention. Wendy gave her a quick report, explaining how Devon's mother had gone home to arrange for child care for an older sibling. Krista was very afraid Devon would end up in PICU before the poor woman could return.

"Krista, the lab is on line one."

She picked up the phone. "This is Krista."

"We have a critical bicarbonate level on Devon Gibson. His bicarb is 9.0."

"Nine point zero?" Krista repeated, writing the number down, knowing it was a dangerously low level. Devon definitely had severe acidosis. "Why don't you give me the rest of the results, too?"

The lab tech ran down the rest of the basic chemistry results. As soon as Krista finished with the lab, she paged Adam again.

"I have the lab results," Krista informed him.

"I'm on my way in," Adam said. "I asked one of my partners to cover my last patient for me. Go ahead and give me the results."

She went down the list, making sure she read each one of the electrolytes correctly. "The lab called with a critical bicarb value of 9.0."

"Yeah, there's also a pretty significant anion gap." Adam's tone was thoughtful. "Stop all Devon's feedings until further notice. Also I want you to start a bicarb drip and check his urine for ketones."

"I understand." Krista wrote everything down, worried she'd forget something. She wanted to ask what he meant by the anion gap, but there wasn't time.

Adam arrived a few minutes later. "How is he?"

"He tested positive for ketones in his urine." Krista handed him the chart so he could read the results for himself. "What underlying disease do you think he might have?"

"Propionic acidosis, which is also known as propio-hyl CoA carboxylase deficiency," he answered absently, reviewing all the laboratory results.

She had no idea what that was, but it sounded serious. She made a mental note to look the disease up when she had a minute. "So what exactly should I be looking for, other than acidosis?"

Adam glanced up at her, his expression grim. "Signs of CNS depression for one thing, sepsis for another. I should have gotten an ammonia level, too."

"I can call and add that on to the previous basic chemistry panel we drew," Krista offered.

"Thanks. If it's as high as I think it is, we are probably going to need to transfer Devon to the PICU."

Using the phone inside Devon's room, she instructed the lab to test the ammonia level. Adam's serious expression gnawed at her.

"This disease, the propionic acidosis, what sort of prognosis are we looking at?"

"Pretty bad," Adam admitted. "With this illness, Devon's body is unable to metabolize certain proteins and amino acids normally. It's a hereditary disease, passed along through recessive genes." His troubled gaze met hers. "I've never seen a patient survive."

Krista sucked in a quick breath. "No. Oh, his poor mother."

"Yeah." Adam sighed and dragged his hands down his face. "I'll have to tell her. Soon."

Krista didn't envy him that task. "I'll stay with you while you talk to her."

"Thanks." He straightened and examined the baby again. "You have the bicarbonate infusion going, right?"

"Yes." Krista felt so helpless, looking down at the sweetly innocent baby with the devastating disease. She couldn't even imagine how it would feel to lose a child so young.

Losing her parents had been bad enough.

"I'd better check on Joy," she murmured, edging toward the door, fighting tears. "Her breathing has been better, but her fever was still high the last time it was checked."

Adam's gaze sharpened with interest. "How high?"

"About at 38.9."

He nodded thoughtfully. "I'd hoped it would have come down by now. Have you seen any results yet from her cerebrospinal fluid?"

"No, but I expect them soon," Krista replied. "I'll look on the computer again."

"All right. I'll stay here with Devon while you check on Joy."

He obviously didn't feel comfortable leaving Devon alone. Not that she could blame him. She was worried about the baby herself, half hoping the infant would need to be transferred to PICU. She'd never lost a young patient yet and didn't want today to be the first time.

Joy was crying when she went in, but immediately quieted down when she picked the baby up.

"I'm here, little one," she said, stroking her finger down the baby's plump cheek. "What's the matter? Are you finally hungry?"

The way Joy squirmed in her arms and gnawed on her fist, she suspected it was time to try the bottle of formula again. She would have loved to feed the baby herself, but Devon needed attention so she called for one of the nursing assistants to help.

When she had safely handed Joy over to the nursing assistant, Rachel, who was more than happy to sit and feed the baby, Krista headed back into Devon's room.

"How is Joy?" Adam asked.

"Fine. Our nursing assistant, Rachel, is feeding her."

"Good." For a moment satisfaction flared in his eyes, then he glanced down at the baby. "Krista, would you call the lab and ask about that ammonia level? I think Devon is getting more lethargic."

"Of course." Once again she picked up the phone and called the lab. In a few minutes she had the ammonia level. "It's high at sixty-five."

"Sixty-five. Normal is less than twenty." Adam frowned. "We need to transfer him to PICU."

"I'm on it." Unable to hide her overwhelming relief, Krista went out to the nurses' station to call the pediatric ICU and the admitting department to let them know about the transfer. As they were in the midst of rolling Devon's crib down the hall, his mother arrived.

"What's going on?" she asked in alarm.

Adam glanced at Krista and she nodded, able to understand his unspoken request. "I'll take Devon over so you can talk to her."

"Thanks." Adam took Mrs Gibson's arm and led her into a quiet corner. Krista could hear the woman sobbing behind her as she continued rolling Devon's crib down the hall.

PICU was located right around the corner from Six South. Devon wasn't the first patient she'd transferred to critical care, but he was by far the sickest.

She did her best to give the attending physician an accurate report on Devon's condition. "Dr Monroe is talking to Devon's mother, but his main concern is lethargy with a serum ammonia level of sixty-five. We've had Devon on the bicarb infusion for almost an hour, and he should have his basic chemistry panel rechecked."

The attending physician nodded. "What's his anion gap?"

Darn, she should have asked Adam to explain it to her. "I'm not sure," she told him. "But here are all his chemistry results. Adam thought the anion gap was significant."

"Yeah." The physician glanced at the numbers, and then nodded. "Eighteen is pretty significant all right. OK, we're going to need to intubate this little guy."

Krista stepped back, watching as the team of PICU nurses and doctors took over Devon's care. A few minutes later Adam brought Devon's mother in, too. With Devon's mother between them, Krista and Adam stood with her until her son had been intubated.

"I need to call my husband," Devon's mother whispered.

Krista kept a supporting arm around her waist as they walked to the nearest phone. After Mrs Gibson placed the call, they were allowed in to see the baby.

Devon looked so defenseless with the breathing tube in his throat. The PICU nurses took Devon's mother under their wing, allowing Adam and Krista to return to the floor.

Sobered by the seriousness of Devon's illness, Krista fell into step beside Adam as they walked down the hall back toward Six South. She couldn't think of a single thing to say that didn't sound trite or placating.

Losing a patient was never easy, not for doctors or nurses. The tense expression on his face tore at her heart. He was truly upset about Devon. As they approached Joy's room, she lightly touched his arm. "I'm sorry, Adam."

He stared down at her hand on his arm and then gave a jerky nod. "I know. There are some diseases medicine just can't fix."

"Yes." Logically she knew he was right. "But that doesn't make it easier, knowing one of your patients may die."

"You're right. Especially considering Devon is so small, he's barely had a chance to live his life." Adam's green eyes glittered with pain, and Krista was taken aback by his fierce expression and the rawness of his tone. "There needs to be a rule—babies never have to die."

CHAPTER FOUR

WHEN Krista's eyes filled with concern, Adam mentally kicked himself for allowing her to see his pain. Normally he didn't have a problem keeping his emotions under control but today it seemed he'd stretched his limits. Krista's kindness made it all too easy to let go, even though he knew better.

He glanced at the rather lopsided Christmas tree in the corner of the patient lounge, not far from Joy's room. The holiday season didn't help—Devon's young face had reminded him too much of his stillborn son.

"Adam?" Krista put her hand on his arm. "Are you all right? Should we go somewhere and talk?"

Krista's earnest expression warmed his heart. He pulled himself together, giving his head a decisive shake. "No, I'm fine. I'd actually like to check on Joy, she's the one bright spot in this day, don't you think?"

She flashed an uncertain smile, dropping her hand. "Yes, I do."

He missed her touch, but told himself to get over it as he picked up Joy's clipboard and led the way into the baby's room. Joy was sitting in an infant seat on top of the crib mattress, no doubt because she'd just finished eating. He glanced down to read the amount listed on the intake and output form. "Two ounces." He grinned with a sense of satisfaction. "She's finally taking more nourishment."

"Two ounces is wonderful." Krista headed straight over to the baby, unbuckling the straps of the infant seat and then lifting Joy against her shoulder. "Her breathing seems better today, too. Did you notice her pulse ox is reading in the mid-nineties?"

"Yeah." He couldn't argue with Krista's assessment. For a moment he watched her, noticing how she held the baby with a natural grace. At times like this he was struck by how different Krista was from her older sister. Danielle may have been gorgeous, but she'd loved to go out, to dance and have fun. She hadn't been thrilled about having their baby. She'd claimed she wasn't ready to be a mother, that she had her whole life ahead of her. The way Krista brushed her cheek against Joy's soft crown, he couldn't imagine she'd feel the same way.

The stirring of desire irked him. He tore his gaze from the image of Krista holding Joy and forced himself to review the rest of Joy's medical record. Her blood results were back, and the antibiotics he'd ordered provided the coverage he needed. Her cerebrospinal fluid was clear—no infection there. Everything was going according to plan.

There was nothing more for him to do for the baby. In a few days Joy would be medically stable enough to be discharged. Assessing her hearing loss might give him a little more time, but he'd have to meet with the social worker. Soon.

"So how has your family been, Adam?" Krista asked.

He was surprised at her abrupt change of subject. "Fine. Alec married Jillian last month and a few months before that my sister Abby married Nick." He was very glad that he and Danielle hadn't made the mistake of getting married. They'd simply been too different.

And he hadn't really loved her. He'd cared about her, but hadn't been deeply in love, the way a man was supposed to love his wife.

The way his father loved his mother.

The knowledge only fueled his guilt. His fault. The accident and everything that followed had been his fault.

"Ah, that explains why Alec looked so happy when I saw him walking down the hall yesterday."

"He is." He shoved aside his feelings of guilt and tried to focus on something else. Like finding Joy's mother. He needed to get in touch with his brother, to see if Alec had any leads. Time was running out and he didn't want to see the baby go into foster-care. There had to be some way to find Joy's mother.

"Danielle sent me an e-mail a couple of days ago. She's doing really well, too." Krista's voice was bright, cheerful. "She absolutely loves London."

How could they find Joy's mother? Look through birth records to see how many baby girls had been born with the first name of Joy? The tactic would only work if Joy's mother had given birth in Milwaukee. And they didn't have an exact date to go by either. Preoccupied, he nodded at Krista. "Good for her. I'm glad Danielle is happy."

"Really?" Krista's surprised expression made him frown.

"Yes. Really." He tore his attention from Joy to Krista. Did she think he harbored ill feelings toward her

sister? He hastened to reassure her. "Danielle and I—
we wanted different things out of life." He didn't miss
the roller-coaster ride of a relationship with Danielle,
but he did still grieve for the loss of their child. The
baby hadn't had a chance at twenty-three weeks gesta-
tion—there had been no way to save him.

He'd briefly considered a funeral, but Danielle
hadn't wanted one. She hadn't wanted anyone to know
about the miscarriage. He'd agreed, mostly because
talking about losing his son had been too painful. So
he hadn't said a word, not even to his family. And from
what he could tell, Danielle hadn't told her own sister
either. What would Krista think if she knew his role in
his son's death?

"That's what Danielle said, too," Krista admitted,
carrying on the conversation as if he wasn't preoccupied with his guilt. "I miss her, but she's living the life
she's always wanted."

Yeah, he could certainly believe that. Danielle hadn't
wanted the baby, yet after the miscarriage she'd furi-
ously blamed him for the accident and the loss of the
baby. He'd sensed her confusion, and had known that
the closeness they'd once shared had ended. She'd been
right. If he hadn't been arguing with her over the future
of their child, he might have seen the truck barreling
through the intersection, heading straight toward them.

He should have been able to avoid the accident.

The sound of Christmas music interrupted his trou-
blesome thoughts. Hospital carolers, he realized as their
singing grew louder.

Krista carried Joy to the doorway, humming along
with the song "Winter Wonderland". He followed, won-

dering where Krista was planning to spend the holiday. He couldn't imagine Danielle would fly home from London, and neither of them had been close to their relatives.

Except for the one aunt—what was her name? Betty? Barbara? Bea? Yes, that was it, Aunt Bea. He'd met the woman a couple of times. Danielle had claimed she was the best out of the bunch. He remembered when Krista had asked for his help—she'd been worried Bea had suffered a small stroke and she'd been right. Even as a student her nursing assessment skills had been excellent.

Was Bea doing better? Would Krista spend a quiet Christmas evening with her aunt? Or did she have to work the holiday? Either way, he didn't like to think of Krista spending the holiday alone.

He glanced at Krista again and easily imagined how she'd enjoy the typical loud, chaotic, Monroe Christmas. Krista would fit in with his family better than Danielle ever had.

The only down side was that if he invited her over, his mother wouldn't understand they were only friends. She'd be so thrilled he'd brought a girl home that she'd start planning another wedding.

And after things had fallen apart with Danielle, he'd realized the truth. He wasn't at all interested in pursuing a serious relationship.

They hurt too much.

Krista was a little disappointed when Adam left minutes after the carolers had finished their song. She understood he was busy. No doubt he'd gone to make rounds on the rest of his patients.

Yet as she admitted a new eighteen-month-old baby, not one of Adam's patients this time, she couldn't help thinking about him. Even the seriousness of Devon's illness couldn't ruin Krista's cheerful mood. She'd been brave enough to broach the subject of Danielle with Adam, and had succeeded in eliminating the awkwardness between them.

She was fairly good at reading people, and Adam hadn't seemed upset when she'd mentioned Danielle. In fact, he'd looked as if he couldn't have cared less what her sister had been up to over the past year.

She was confident he didn't still love her sister.

Yet his reaction after Devon's transfer to the PICU nagged at her. He'd seemed more upset than she'd have thought he would have been over the situation. Unless he was just the sort of doctor to take his patient's well-being seriously to heart? Maybe. Preparing Devon's mother for the potential worst-case scenario couldn't have been easy. Maybe Adam had become a pediatrician because the likelihood of losing his patients was less likely than in the adult world.

As Krista finished her shift and headed home, she realized that there were lots of things about Adam Monroe she didn't know. She didn't know what had drawn him to medicine, or to pediatrics in particular. She didn't know what his plans were for the future.

And realized how much she wanted to find out.

The next day she was off work, so she ran dozens of errands, beginning the task of Christmas shopping. Krista had been designated to buy the gifts for the babies on the unit, spending the money all the Six South staff had contributed. With her arms laden with bags of gifts, many of them for Joy, she didn't see Adam's younger sister, Abby, until she practically ran the woman over.

"Krista? Is that you?" Abby asked, once they'd disentangled themselves and their packages. "It's been years since I saw you last. How are you?"

"Great, thanks." She'd gone to high school with Abby, but instead of going straight to college, like Abby had, she'd worked for several years to earn money for tuition. Her parents had died when she and Danielle had been young, and hadn't thought about practical things like life insurance. She didn't blame them— what young couple expected to die in a car crash? "I heard you're happily married now, to a guy named Nick."

Abby's jaw dropped. "Yes. Who told you?"

Krista laughed. "Adam. I ran into him, working at Children's Memorial Hospital."

"Ah, that explains it." Abby's smile broadened. "You're a nurse, too? So am I. That's how I met Nick, actually. He's a doctor, a rehab specialist."

"You look wonderful, Abby. Married life obviously agrees with you." Krista was genuinely pleased. Abby had always been nice to her during those horrible years of high school. When many of the kids had made fun of her because she hadn't had money or nice clothes, Abby had befriended her anyway. They'd drifted apart once Abby had gone off to college while Krista had worked two jobs to save money.

"So you're working with Adam." Abby's curious tone wasn't lost on Krista.

"Yes, but get that look out of your eyes—he thinks of me like a sister." No matter how much she wished he didn't. "We shared an interesting patient, though, a baby girl who was abandoned in Adam's waiting room."

"I heard about her. Joy, right? Alec mentioned it. Sad situation, but I'm sure if her mother doesn't return, the baby will be adopted fast."

"Actually, maybe not. We think she might be deaf."

"The poor thing." Abby glanced down at her watch. "I wish we could do lunch and talk more about this but I really have to run. I promised to watch Shelby, Alec's daughter, and need to be home by noon. Maybe another time?"

"I'd like that." Krista smiled and hefted her bags once, again. "Take care, Abby."

"You, too, Krista. Please, keep in touch." Abby took off at a fast pace, making Krista sense her friend was running late. She had far more bags to lug through the mall, so she followed more slowly. When she passed a bookstore, she turned inside.

Meandering her way down the aisles, she finally found what she was looking for. A book on sign language. Even if Joy did qualify for a cochlear trans-plant, there was no guarantee the procedure would work. Whoever eventually adopted Joy would have to learn sign language in order to help communicate with the girl.

Krista bought the book, adding the item to her numerous bags. Slowly she made her way out of the mall, trudging through the slush to her car parked far from the entrance.

At home, a small one-bedroom apartment she'd

moved into after Danielle had taken off for London, she spent time wrapping the Christmas gifts she'd purchased for the children. Then took the book on sign language and began looking through the pictures explaining simple words and phrases.

Although she knew there was a very real possibility Joy's mother might make herself known, she couldn't shake the idea of possibly caring for the baby herself. A full adoption took a long time, but she'd learned about being a temporary receiving home with one of her last cases, a baby whose mother had been severely ill and hospitalized for months. Krista had actually started the application, but hadn't completed the process.

Now she wished she had. She couldn't stand the thought of sending Joy into the foster system.

After their parents had died, she and Danielle had ended up in a foster-home. It had been a horrible experience. There had been lots of kids and the woman who'd opened her home to them hadn't bothered to learn anyone's names, calling them all nicknames based on how they'd looked. She'd referred to Krista as Mouse, for her mousy brown hair, while Danielle had been dubbed the Wild Child. The woman hadn't physically hurt them or anything, but she had demanded countless chores be done, not least of which consisted of the older kids taking care of the younger ones.

Krista hadn't minded, but Danielle, in her typical fashion, had rebelled. Thankfully the foster-home hadn't lasted long, but then their relatives had started fighting over who had to take care of them, shunting them off to one house after the other. It had taken years for them to find Aunt Bea, who'd actually accepted them for who they were.

She knew what it was like not to be wanted. To be considered a burden. And she refused to allow Joy to feel that way.

Glancing down at the book, she mimicked the hand gestures and began to practice the alphabet.

A, B, C, D…

Adam couldn't get Krista out of his mind. He'd put in a full day at Pediatric Health before dashing to the hospital to go on rounds of his patients. He was disappointed he didn't see Krista in Joy's room. After he'd finished, he'd returned to the clinic to catch up on paperwork. The long, empty evening stretched ahead of him.

How had he missed Krista? And why had missing her ruined his evening?

His parents had asked him over for dinner, so he'd decided to go, mostly because he was too lazy to cook something for himself and, besides, he really needed to see how his mother was coming along.

His mother had broken her hip two years ago, and although she was healed and moving independently, he was still a little worried about her. She'd slowed down over the past two years and walked carefully, as if her joints ached. He'd mentioned the possibility of arthritis to Abby's husband, Nick, and he'd agreed that she should probably be seen.

But being the stubborn woman she was, she'd refused. Living with doctors and nurses was annoying, she'd said. They were always seeing one illness or another when nothing was wrong. She was absolutely fine.

He didn't believe her, but what could he do, force her to be evaluated? Alec had thought so, had even tried to push Jillian to talk to her, but the women had stuck together. Jillian had refused, telling Alec his mother's health was none of his business.

Adam didn't agree but, considering his hands were tied, there wasn't much he could do except make sure he took frequent trips home to watch her closely for himself.

When he'd finished checking lab results and radiology reports, making his final notes in the various records, he stood and stacked the charts he'd been working on in a neat pile, so Doris wouldn't threaten to quit when she came in the next morning. The office was empty as everyone else had gone home already. The situation wasn't unusual. Out of the three partners in his practice, he was the only single guy left. There'd never been a reason to rush home.

Thinking of his empty condo reminded him again of Krista. Considering he'd once only thought of her as a younger sister, she was occupying his thoughts more than she should.

So what if she was empathetic, kind and considerate? So what if she was beautiful in a quiet, down-to-earth way? She deserved someone better, a guy who could love her and marry her. Give her a family. He'd watched her with Joy—she was definitely a woman who wanted a family.

And he was a man who wasn't crazy enough to get involved in a complicated relationship again.

Scowling, he pulled on his leather coat and gloves, before heading outside. His clinic had a back door for the staff, and he pulled the door shut behind him, making sure it was securely locked. December in Wisconsin was cold and dark. As he walked round the corner of the building, he saw a woman standing in front of the Pediatric Health Clinic front door, her face pressed up against the glass.

Curious, he stepped closer. What was she looking at? She must have noticed his reflection in the glass because she suddenly spun around, giving him a quick impression of a woman's pale, wan face surrounded by a dark blue scarf, before she hurried off in the opposite direction.

"Hey!" he called out to her, wondering if she'd come because she'd thought the clinic was still open. "Are you all right? Do you need medical help?"

The mystery woman acted as if she didn't hear him. He started off after her, but then stopped when she went straight to the bus stop. She rubbed her bare hands together and blew into them as if to warm her fingers.

She was alone. She hadn't brought a child to the clinic to be evaluated.

He turned to walk back to his car, the cold wind cutting through his coat. It wasn't until he had the car warmed up and had pulled out onto the highway toward his parents' house that he considered the odd encounter in more detail.

The woman had been wearing a rather thin coat, considering the temperature outside was well below zero. She'd had the scarf tucked around her face, but her fingers had been bare, lacking the protection of warm gloves. She'd dressed as if she didn't have much money, and she couldn't have owned a car, the way she'd gone straight to the bus stop.

Why was the woman peering into his clinic?

Was it possible she was Joy's mother?

CHAPTER FIVE

ADAM wished he'd thought to use his cellphone camera to get a picture of the woman for Alec. He had a pretty vivid image of her in his head, though, and he mentally reviewed her description as he headed towards his parents' for dinner, knowing Alec would want details.

After parking his car on the street in front of his parents' house, he strode inside and found his family gathered in the kitchen. "Hi, Mom, Dad." Crossing the room, he gave his mother a hug and a kiss, scanning the room for Alec. "How are you?"

"Good." She gave him an easy smile, and he was glad to note she didn't look strained or exhausted.

He raised a brow, searching her expression for the truth. "Are you sure? How's your hip? Giving you any pain?"

"No pain. My hip is fine. Look, Austin surprised us with a visit, too." His mother appeared to be thrilled with the prospect of cooking for so many of his siblings. "Abe." She turned to his father, a large, gentle man who was the rock in their family. "Take everyone into the living room and get them something to drink, would you? There's plenty of wine. Dinner will be ready in a half-hour or so."

"You heard your mother." Abe's deep voice boomed through the kitchen. "Let me know if you want something other than wine."

Dismissed from the kitchen, Adam clapped his younger brother Austin on the back as they followed their father into the living room. "Hey, Austin," he greeted him. "I haven't seen you in months. How's the smoke-jumping?"

"Going as well as can be expected." Austin didn't smile and the expression in his brother's eyes reflected his somber mood. "The fire in Esperanza is finally out, at least."

Austin had trained as a firefighter and paramedic, but last year had joined the smoke-jumping team so he could fight wildfires in California. Adam could tell something had happened, something serious, but a crowded room didn't seem the appropriate time or place to ask.

"Where's Alec?" he asked, taking a glass of red wine his father offered him.

"He can't make it." Abby spoke up, perching on the arm of the sofa where her husband was seated. "Shelby has a cold, so he and Jillian are staying home." Abby leaned into Nick when he wrapped an arm around her waist. "Hey, Adam, guess who I ran into today?"

He rolled his eyes, hiding his disappointment over Alec's absence. He'd have to call Alec to let him know about the mystery woman. "Why don't you just tell me instead of making me guess?"

"Dinner's almost ready." Their mother entered the room, taking the glass of wine his father offered her. He was happy to see there was no hesitation in his mother's gait. Maybe she really was doing better after all.

"Krista Vaughn." Abby's tone was light, teasing. "She told me she's a nurse at Children's Memorial. Said she's working with you on a patient, that abandoned baby you told us about."

"Yeah." He took a hasty sip of his wine and cursed under his breath when he saw his mother's eyes widen, gleaming with interest. "She's a nice kid."

"Kid?" Abby's eyebrows rose with barely repressed indignation.

Nick groaned and shook his head. "Now you've done it," he muttered.

"Excuse me?" Abby's voice rose as she continued, "Krista and I went to high school together, so you'd better rephrase that, buster. We are not kids. We're women."

When Krista had touched his arm, the desire that had shot through him had made him all too aware of her as a woman, but he tried again. "Hey, that's my point—you're both the same age. You're my kid sister. I've always thought of Krista as another kid sister."

"Hrmph." Abby was clearly irritated with him.

"Austin, help me out here," he cajoled his brother.

Austin still didn't smile. "I remember Krista, she was a few years behind me in high school. She was quiet and shy, a little plain but with nice curves in all the right places."

"She's not plain." His automatic denial burst out before he could bite his tongue. Austin was right, though, about her curves. Krista wasn't willow-thin like Danielle, she had very nice curves. Not that her figure was any of his business. What was wrong with him? Why couldn't he keep Krista tucked in the little-sister box where she belonged?

"You'd hardly recognize her, Austin," Abby agreed. "*I* almost didn't realize who she was at first. She's cut her hair short and highlighted it. She wears contacts now, or had laser surgery, I don't know which. She's very pretty."

"Hmm, maybe I should give her a call," Austin mused, pursing his lips. "I wouldn't mind taking her out while I'm home."

What? Adam straightened in his seat, glaring at his brother slouched on the sofa. "She's not the sort of girl you use for a quick fling, Austin. Unless you're moving back home for good?"

"No." Austin's eyes clouded over. "I'm only home until after the holidays."

Austin had been gone for months, and it sounded like he'd be heading back to California again soon. Adam frowned, not liking the way his once carefree younger brother seemed to be carrying the weight of the world on his shoulders.

Annoyed with the idea of Austin asking Krista out, he stood and pulled out his cellphone, walking toward the kitchen as he dialed Alec.

"Hey," he greeted his brother. "How's Shelby?"

"Miserable." Alec sighed. "Upset that we wouldn't let her come to dinner."

"Tell her Grandma and Grandpa will have another dinner next week. I'm sure Mom won't mind." He cleared his throat and got straight to the point. "I called because I saw a woman peering into the window of Pediatric Health when I left this evening. When I called out to her, she hurried off. I think it's possible she could be Joy's mother."

"Describe her for me," Alec instructed.

Adam included every detail he could remember as he described the woman and the sequence of events. "I guess what bothered me the most was the way she wouldn't even talk to me, just took off."

"Are you sure she wasn't just window-shopping?" Alec asked. "Seriously, Adam, just because she looked as if she might not have a lot of money doesn't mean she's Joy's mother."

"There aren't any stores in the building we rent, Alec. There's an adult clinic, a pediatric clinic and a dentist office. Do you think she was window-shopping for dentures?"

"All right, I'll see what I can do. If you see her again, let me know."

"I will. Thanks, Alec." Adam hung up and glanced back at where Abby, Nick and Austin were still talking. His gaze zeroed in on his brother. Austin was leaner than he remembered, he'd lost weight over the past nine months. Smoke-jumping must be physically demanding. Emotionally, too, if Austin's shuttered expression was anything to go by.

Had he been serious about asking Krista out? Nah, Adam couldn't believe it. Then again, why not? Austin looked so somber, maybe his younger brother needed a little fun. Krista was closer to his age, she'd probably say yes.

His mind continued to dwell on the image of his brother and Krista together. If Austin did ask Krista out, she'd probably touch his arm and offer to talk about his troubles, too. Austin would appreciate her comforting presence, may even open up to Krista about whatever had happened to him in California.

Damn. He didn't like the flash of jealousy that gripped him by the throat and squeezed tight.

Didn't like it at all.

Krista shot out of bed when her phone rang. For a moment she stared, disoriented, until she realized she was at home on her day off.

"Hello?"

"Krista?" Melanie, her boss from Six South, was on the line. "Do you think you could come in for a few hours? Emma's son is sick and she needs to go home."

"Ah, sure." She grimaced, knowing she had things to do but unable to bring herself to say no. Besides, the patients needed someone to care for them. She glanced at the clock, realizing it was later than she'd thought, almost nine in the morning. "I can be there in an hour."

"Great, thanks Krista." Melanie hung up, no doubt worried she'd change her mind.

As she headed for the shower, the remnants of her dream drifted from her subconscious. She'd been in the car with Adam, but it had been the night when she'd called home, breathless and crying, desperately needing a ride. Adam had answered her sister's cellphone and had offered to come get her because Danielle had been sick with a migraine.

His quiet strength and concern had helped her to calm down. As if he'd sensed she needed time, Adam hadn't rushed but had driven slowly through the streets, gently probing her about what had happened. She'd explained how Robert had driven to his place, instead of taking her back to her apartment. When she'd protested, he insisted he'd only forgotten his wallet and would be right back. She'd waited outside, standing beside his car. When he'd returned, he'd pulled her close for a kiss. At first she hadn't minded, but then he'd pressed her against the car, kissing her hard. When she'd tried to break away, he wouldn't let her go. She'd panicked, shoving at his chest, and he'd finally stopped kissing her and grabbed her shoulders, demanding to know what her problem was. His tight grasp had hurt and she'd kicked him in the groin and taken off, running.

She felt foolish for allowing things to spiral out of control. Adam had been angry on her behalf, demanding to know the guy's last name and how well she knew him. She'd only gone out with Robert once before and there hadn't been any problems. He had been a friend of a friend, but the incident had scared her enough that she'd stopped dating for a while.

Adam had driven her home, walking with her up to the apartment she'd shared with Danielle and giving her a brotherly hug once inside. He'd wanted her to go to the police but she'd refused. Deep down, she'd suspected the incident had been her fault, that she'd somehow given Robert the wrong impression or just simply blown the whole thing out of proportion.

Why she'd dreamed about that night now, she didn't know. Adam had been kind and gentle. Seeing him again shouldn't have brought back those memories of that night. Adam had been there for her. He'd been as protective as if he'd been her big brother, wanting to beat up the guy who'd hurt her.

Maybe that was it, she thought as she headed in to work. She'd dreamed about that night because Adam had treated her kindly, like an older brother. There was no reason to think Adam's feelings toward her had changed.

She'd always liked Adam, more than she should have. The morning after he'd rescued her, Danielle had complained about having to go to dinner at Adam's parents' house, making Krista feel angry. Although she'd known her sister had just been mouthing off, that family gatherings had driven Danielle crazy, she had still spent the rest of the day stewing over how Danielle didn't deserve Adam.

Krista tucked the memories away as she rode the elevator to the sixth floor. She'd been so worried Adam was still hung up on her sister that she'd ignored the obvious. What really mattered was how Adam felt toward her. Her dream reminded her how he'd once cared about her as a sister. He was a good doctor and she was his colleague. Logically, she knew their relationship was nothing more than simple friendship.

And if she'd always wished for more, it was her problem, not his.

"Thanks for coming in, Krista." Melanie smiled at her when she arrived on the unit. "Would you mind taking over Emma's assignment? Joy is one of her patients."

"No problem." Obviously, her boss had figured out how attached she'd become to baby Joy. She found Emma and listened to the run-down of her three patients.

"Little Joseph has been diagnosed with mumps, he's just shy of two years old, his mother has several other kids at home and the father is working tons of hours to make ends meet, so she's not around as much. Britney is a seven-month-old being evaluated for failure to thrive. Joy is doing very well—some auditory testing will be done today."

"Sounds good." One of the reasons Krista liked this unit was because there was always a wide variety of illnesses to learn about. And normally the babies weren't so sick, although Devon had been the exception.

She'd barely reviewed all the orders when Adam strolled in. Her chest tightened when she looked at him. He looked incredibly handsome in a shirt, tie, dress trousers and white lab coat. She prayed her reaction wasn't obvious. "Hi, Adam."

"Krista, how are you?"

"Fine, thanks. Are you here to see Joy?" She knew he wasn't the attending physician on either of her other two patients.

"Yes, I ordered some preliminary auditory testing for her today." He smiled and fell into step beside her as they walked into Joy's room. "I'm anxious to see the results."

"They haven't called for her yet," Krista said in an apologetic tone. "Do you want me to see if I can get her moved up on the schedule?"

"No, it's not a big deal. I'm sure you're busy." Adam glanced down at Joy. Krista had left the baby propped upright in the infant seat, still in the croup tent, after she'd taken her bottle.

Krista was busy, but felt bad that he'd come all the way in to see test results for tests that hadn't even been done yet. "Actually, I have to check on my other patients. Joseph is doing all right, but Britney didn't eat very well this morning."

"Britney Meyer?" Adam asked, turning to face her.

When she nodded, he went on, "I need to examine her, too. My partner is out of town for the day at his wife's grandfather's funeral. I'm covering his patients."

She should have remembered Rick Johnson was Adam's partner. After months of not having any of Adam's patients, she thought it was amazing she seemed to be interacting with him on almost every shift she worked at the moment.

"Would you like to examine Joy first, or go and see Britney?"

"Joy seems to be doing fine, if you're worried about Britney, we'd better see her first."

She appreciated how he apparently trusted her professional nursing judgment. "All right, Britney is in room 620, just down the hall."

"How much did she take this morning?" Adam asked, as they made the short trip down the hall.

"Just three ounces, not nearly enough for a seven-month-old. And she doesn't like to eat solid food at all. We tried a little fruit and cereal this morning but she wasn't interested."

"Hmm." Adam frowned. "When was she admitted?"

"Last evening, I guess. I don't think they've ordered much in the way of tests for her." Krista approached the crib, dropping the side so Adam could get access to Britney. The phone on her hip rang, and she turned from him to answer it.

"This is the auditory lab. We're ready for Joy Smith," the woman said.

"All right." Krista hung up her phone and glanced at Adam. "I have to take Joy downstairs. Is there anything you need for Britney before I go?"

"No, I'm fine. Go ahead, I'm sure I'll catch up with you later."

She nodded and went to fetch Joy. She stayed with the baby through the testing, and by the time she returned Joy to her room, it was close to lunchtime. She checked on Britney and squashed her disappointment when she discovered Adam had left. He'd written a page of orders, though, so she quickly signed them off and began getting the tasks completed. She was late for her lunch-break because she took the time to make sure Britney's IV fluids were started before heading down to the cafeteria.

"Shirley?" she called, seeing the social worker for Six South ahead of her in the queue. "Can I ask you a few questions over lunch?"

"Sure." Shirley waited for Krista to catch up and then found a small table for the two of them to sit. "What's wrong? Is this about Joy?"

"Yes, actually, it is," Krista confessed. She toyed with her grilled chicken salad. "Remember a few months back, when I applied to be a temporary receiving home for foster-kids?"

"I remember." Shirley dug into her cheeseburger with gusto.

"I know it's a six-week process to get approved, but as I've already done the paperwork, the classes and the interview, do you think they would push the application through?"

After she swallowed, Shirley shrugged. "It might work. Although, if I remember correctly, the one concern they had during your application process was your single-bedroom apartment. Has that changed in the past two months?"

"No." She'd forgotten that part. They had strongly recommended she upgrade to a two-bedroom place. "But I could look into it. Maybe there's something opening up in my building." She couldn't afford to break her lease.

"Please, do." Shirley gave her hand a quick squeeze. "I'll give you another reference if you need one. And if it doesn't work out, we'll make sure we place Joy in a good home. She'll be fine."

"Yeah. I know." Krista tried to smile, but the rest of her appetite had vanished. Shirley finished her lunch just as her pager went off. She stopped at the phone on her way out.

Krista followed more slowly. She'd really liked the idea of taking Joy in as a temporary receiving home, at least until her mother was found. And if her mother wasn't found, maybe she'd even be in a position to adopt her. Completely dejected, she made her way to the elevators.

"Krista?" A familiar male voice caused her to glance up. Adam walked toward her, his brow puckered in a tiny frown as he reached out to take her arm. "What is it? What's wrong?"

"Nothing is wrong." She didn't want Adam to know about her financial woes. She didn't even know what he'd think of her wanting to eventually adopt Joy. Heck, it wasn't as if she had lots of extra money to support a child.

Just an abundance of love.

"Don't tell me nothing is wrong." Adam clearly wasn't buying her story. "You look just like the night I picked you up after that jerk attacked you. Talk to me, Krista. Tell me what's made you so upset."

CHAPTER SIX

KRISTA was stunned to realize how well Adam could read her. She wasn't at all sure she liked knowing her feelings were so transparent. Especially when she didn't know as much about him. As nice as he was, he seemed to hold his inner emotions close, unwilling to share them.

Like after Devon's transfer to PICU. Something had been bothering him, but he'd refused to tell her what.

He lightly grasped her arm, his green eyes dark with suppressed anger. "Did some guy come on to you? Or threaten you? What happened?"

"No, it's nothing like that." Good grief, how embarrassing to know he'd jumped to the worst conclusion possible. She ducked her head to hide her pink cheeks. "Really, Adam, nothing is wrong. I received a bit of disheartening news, that's all."

He stared at her for a long moment, silently asking what the disheartening news was. Should she tell him? There was no reason to keep her desire to be a temporary receiving home for emergency foster-care a secret yet she was loath to open herself up to his scrutiny.

"Code blue, Six South. Code blue, Six South."

When the PA announcement came on, Krista's heart

jumped as if someone had poked her with a sharp stick. When Adam's eyes widened in horror, she knew he thought the same thing.

"Joy!"

Adam didn't answer but dashed for the nearest stairwell. She followed close on his heels. Adam wasn't part of the code blue response team and neither was she, yet that fact didn't stop her from making a valorous attempt to keep up as they took the stairs.

Her lungs felt as if they might cave from the pressure when they finally reached the sixth floor. They were both huffing and puffing as they burst through the door, heading down the hall in time to see a blue code cart being wheeled into a room.

Not Joy's room, thank heavens.

Her step faltered. Britney's room? No. Oh, dear God, no. She pushed her way past the people standing in the doorway to see if Jenny Spritz, the nurse who'd agreed to cover her patients while she went to lunch, was there. Jenny stood at the opposite side of the room, her eyes full of apology. "What happened?" she asked.

"I tried to feed her again and she suddenly turned blue." Jennifer was a new nurse, too, had actually gone through the same orientation program as Krista had. She looked frazzled. "I didn't know what to do."

"Calling a code blue was the right thing to do." Adam spoke up. Krista glanced at him, thankful he was there. This was the first time any of her patients had arrested and she hadn't even been there. Adam's gaze swept the room. "Who's leading this code?"

"I am," one of the ED doctors answered. Krista recognized him as Dr Kevin Irvine. "So far we've been able to ventilate with the ambu-bag and mask and, we were just deciding whether or not she needed to be intubated."

"I'm covering for the attending physician of record," Adam said in an authoritative tone. "Krista, did we get the chest X-ray I ordered?"

"Yes." Britney's pulse ox remained on the low side at 88 per cent so she understood his concern. Her tone was a tad defensive. "I carried out all the orders you wrote, before I went to lunch."

Adam nodded and she realized maybe he wasn't questioning her nursing care. "I know. I need to see the results. Keep bagging her unless her pulse ox drops below 85 per cent and I'll be right back."

He disappeared and she knew he was going down the hall to the X-ray viewing machine. Actual film wasn't used any more. All the images were digital, making it easy to see the results on designated computer screens.

She watched helplessly as Kevin Irvine continued to gently breathe for Britney with the ambu-bag. Was there something she'd missed while caring for Britney? Some subtle sign that may have foreshadowed her changing condition? Something a more experienced nurse may have picked up on sooner?

Adam strode back into the room. "She has a severe lung deformity. Her pulmonary artery is constricted to the point where it looks almost completely obliterated. Krista, get a cardiothoracic surgeon in here, now."

She reached for the phone in Britney's room to make the call as Adam continued addressing the team. "Kevin, she needs to be intubated as soon as possible."

After calling the hospital operator to request the cardiothoracic surgeon on call be paged, she watched the events unfold. She wasn't part of the emergency response team, so she couldn't do much to help. The phone rang and she pounced on it, quickly filling the surgeon in on what was happening.

"Dr Ben Christenson is on his way." She tried to keep her voice from shaking. "And I've called to reserve a PICU bed for her."

"Good." Adam's gaze was riveted on the team working over Britney. She glanced at the portable heart monitor over the baby's head and her stomach dropped when she noticed Britney's heart rate was rising at a steady rate.

Adam saw it, too. "Her pulse is well over two hundred. As soon as you're finished with the breathing tube, you'll need to cardiovert her."

"I'm finished, just need to verify placement." Before Kevin had finished speaking Adam had pulled his stethoscope out and was listening to Britney's lungs. Krista leaned over to place the small end-tital carbon dioxide detector on the end of the breathing tube. "Good color change," she announced for everyone to hear.

"The tube is in." Adam took his stethoscope out of his ears. "Get ready to cardiovert."

Ben Christenson walked in. "What's going on?"

Adam glanced up. "Chest X-ray from about two hours ago shows a severely constricted pulmonary artery."

"What's her name?"

"Britney Meyer. Her chest image should still be up on the screen."

The surgeon left the room, presumably to see the X-ray for himself. Krista felt sick when Dr Irvine shocked Britney out of her fast heart rate. She never should have left the unit to go to lunch. Ben returned. "Get her over to PICU, I'll call the OR and get the team ready." He frowned, looking over the people standing in the room. "Where's her mother?"

She sucked in a quick breath. How could she have forgotten about Britney's mother? "I'll call her." She reached for the phone and, using the information on her clipboard, dialed Britney's mother.

"Hello?"

"Mrs Meyer? This is Krista from Children's Memorial calling. Britney has taken a turn for the worse. She's OK," she hastened to reassure Mrs Meyer, "but the surgeon is here and needs to talk to you." She handed the phone to Ben Christenson.

As the surgeon explained the situation, Krista pitched in to help the code team prepare to transfer Britney to PICU. Britney's mom must have given permission for the surgery because Ben hung up the phone and filled out an OR consent form.

"Two transfers to the PICU over the course of four days isn't a very good track record," Adam muttered. Krista could only agree. The only bright spot in her day was seeing Devon's name was still on the whiteboard census of PICU, which meant he was still hanging in there.

She held herself together long enough to get Britney settled. Bitter guilt coated her tongue and as soon as possible she escaped.

"Krista?" Adam called. She ignored him, but he caught up to her and took her arm. She shrugged him off, knowing she was on the verge of losing control. "Krista, wait."

"Don't." She stopped and swung toward him. "I'm responsible for this. I left her alone."

"You didn't leave her alone, you left her in another nurse's care. You need to eat, too."

She wished she could believe him, but knew better. He pulled her into a small consulting room and closed the door behind them. Her eyes burned with unshed tears. "It's my fault if she dies."

"Krista, that's not true." He pulled her into his arms and, heaven help her, she leaned against him, needing to absorb some of his strength. She buried her face in the warmth of his chest and inhaled his comforting, musky scent. "Nothing you did caused her pulmonary artery constriction. If you want the truth, there should have been a better physical examination and follow-up prior to her admission. Rick Johnson didn't tell me much, just that he thought there might be some bonding issues between the mother and the baby."

"But maybe if I had stayed, I would have noticed her distress quicker." Her voice was muffled against his shirt. "Maybe I could have prevented the respiratory arrest."

He tunneled his fingers through her hair, cradling her head and lifting her face, forcing her to meet his gaze. His green eyes were dark with compassion and understanding. "Krista, Britney needs surgery. Noticing her distress any sooner wouldn't have made any difference."

"But—" she started to protest, but he leaned forward and covered her mouth with his.

Effectively silencing her protest.

His mouth was warm and she didn't have the strength to resist. He kissed her gently, as if she were fragile and might break. She opened her mouth to welcome him in, wanting more despite the inopportune timing. When she sensed he was easing away she slid her arms around his neck to hold onto the moment for a little longer. For years she'd dreamed of his kiss, but the reality was so much better than her imagination. Adam tasted wonderful, like a mixture of peppermint and chocolate, two of her favorite flavors.

Eventually, he broke off the kiss, breathing deeply. "Krista," he murmured, resting his forehead against hers. "As much as I wish we could stay, we need to get back to the unit."

He was right. Although her shift was just about over, she pulled away, knowing she could get into trouble for being there with him. "Yes. I need to check on Joy."

"Wait." He stopped her when she turned away, reaching for the door. Reluctantly, she glanced back at him. "Krista, I need to know you're all right. Not just about Britney, but about what just happened. I didn't scare you, did I?"

Scare her? Did he really think that she was haunted by the past? Her expression softened. "No, Adam. You didn't scare me."

"Good." He smiled, although she could see uncertainty on his face. "Let's check on Joy."

She nodded, knowing he was being considerate to come with her. Trying to gather her scattered thoughts, she silently cursed the tingling awareness that still invaded her limbs.

Hiding her feelings for Adam was not going to be easy if he ever kissed her like that again.

In fact, she'd have trouble stopping at a single kiss.

Adam held his physical response in check as he walked to Joy's room with Krista. He'd kissed her intimately, sizzling need obliterating his common sense, making him forget how she'd once been frightened by a man. Ending the kiss had taken every ounce of control he possessed, especially when he'd wanted nothing more than to repeat the entire experience again.

They entered Joy's room to find Jenny there, watching over the baby. As Krista hurried forward, he realized his plan to avoid thinking of Krista as a woman was doomed to failure. Physical need still clawed at him and he couldn't remember ever feeling quite this possessive toward any woman in his life.

He was attracted to Krista and he was damned if he'd stand by and let Austin ask her out. The sooner Austin realized Krista was off limits, the better.

"Krista, I'm so sorry," Jenny said, casting a worried glance toward Adam. "I didn't mean for anything to happen to Britney, I swear."

"It's not your fault, Jen," Krista assured her. "I've been feeling guilty, too, but Adam convinced me Britney's problem is her pulmonary artery. She needs surgery to fix the constriction. Neither of us could have prevented the condition. She was probably born with it." She glanced over at Adam, silently asking for confirmation.

"She was definitely born with it," he agreed. "Sometimes babies adapt to their environments too well. Her artery constriction probably became more of a problem once she grew older and more active."

"I hope you're right." Jenny didn't look convinced. "I felt sick the whole time the code team was there. Maybe I wasn't meant to be a pediatric nurse."

"I've had doubts about my choice, too," Krista said in a low tone. Adam imagined she'd felt the same way Jenny had when Devon had needed to be transferred to PICU. "But apart from medical emergencies, I love being a pediatric nurse." He was glad she seemed to have shaken off her guilt as she stepped closer to Jenny. "Think about it, Jen, does any nurse like seeing their patient take a turn for the worse? Sometimes it happens, but it's no reason to give up your career."

"Maybe you're right." Jen's expression lightened as she flashed a small smile. "I just felt so awful, as if I let you down."

"You didn't." Krista glanced at Adam and he nodded encouragingly. "I felt awful, too, because I left you short-handed to eat lunch."

Apparently it was the right thing to say because Jenny laughed and shook her head. "We're a pair, aren't we?"

"Yeah." Krista smiled at Joy, who was looking brightly around the room. "Thanks for keeping an eye on her for me."

"You're welcome. I'm glad our shift is over." Jenny made her way toward the door. "While you were transferring Britney to PICU, I gave Gretchen report on Joy, so you're free to go unless you have something to add."

Adam was glad Krista's grueling shift was over. "Have her auditory results come back yet?"

"I haven't looked for them yet," Jenny admitted.

"Don't worry, I'll do it." He saw Krista gazing down at Joy and decided maybe she needed a few minutes alone. He went outside to look over the chart.

Jenny paused next to him. "Did you have any other questions?"

Adam shook his head. "No, thanks. Go home, have a good evening."

"I'll try." She turned and left.

He read the results, thinking he was prepared, but he wasn't. The results weren't good. After a few minutes, reviewing Joy's records, he went back into the room.

And found Krista cradling the baby against her chest. "How are you, sweetie?" she crooned, pressing a kiss on top of Joy's soft head. "I feel as if I neglected you today."

Hovering in the doorway, he watched as she sat in the rocker and held the baby on her knees so Joy was facing her. He'd noticed Joy was very animated now that she was feeling better, making funny facial expressions while she waved her arms in uncoordinated movements.

"Aren't you just the cutest thing?" Krista asked, smiling at the baby.

He stepped further into the room. "Her auditory test results have confirmed a pretty significant hearing loss, in the 85 to 90 per cent range, so she can't hear you."

Krista's startled glance met his. "I know. During the test I could see she didn't react to the sounds except for maybe to the very highest-pitched ones. But I read that it's important to talk to deaf children face to face so they can eventually learn how to lip-read."

She'd been reading up on deafness in children? He advanced into the room, unable to tear his gaze from the beautiful picture they made together. Watching

Krista interact with Joy, he suspected she was already getting emotionally involved with the baby.

"So I guess she'll need a cochlear implant," Krista said.

"Yes, when she's eligible for surgery, at twelve months or so." He knew a cochlear transplant was only the beginning. Joy would need lots of extra care, special schools, speech therapy, and so on. Was he crazy to search so hard for Joy's mother? So far, if Alec had come up with anything on his mystery woman, he hadn't told Adam about it. And even if they did find her, maybe she really couldn't afford all of this. For all he knew, she didn't even have basic medical coverage.

Yet he firmly believed the child needed to be with her mother. And the rapt expression on Krista's face bothered him. "Wasn't your shift over at three-thirty?" he asked.

"Yes. I'm off duty, don't worry." Her defensive tone grated on his nerves.

"I'm not worried about your work ethic, Krista." He frowned. "I'm worried you're getting too attached to her."

"Joy. Her name is Joy." Her defiant gaze met his. "I was hoping to take Joy in, provide a temporary receiving home for her."

"Really?" He couldn't hide his shock at the news.

"Yes. A similar situation came up a couple of months ago with a baby who needed a temporary home, and I went through the whole application process. I was close to being approved, but there was one recommendation they'd made and I haven't taken care of it yet."

This must have been part of her bad news. He didn't know what to say. Should he tell her he might have found Joy's mother? Or wait until he knew for sure? His cellphone rang and he recognized his brother's number. Did Alec have information? "Hello?"

"Hi, Uncle Adam." Shelby's childish voice made him smile.

"Hi yourself. How are you feeling?"

"I'm fine. I was fine before, too, but Daddy wouldn't listen to me. He and Mommy ganged up on me." Her indignant tone made him laugh.

"I think you need a baby brother or baby sister so that one day you can gang up on your parents and even up the odds a bit."

"Me, too," she confided. "Anyways, I'm supposed to tell you there's a family dinner at Grandma's house this Sunday. Will you come? Please?"

He watched Krista with Joy and knew she was listening to his one-sided conversation. Memories of their heated kiss made his groin tighten. "Sure. Tell Grandma I'd love to come."

"Goody!" Shelby shrilled in his ear. He pulled the phone away to salvage his eardrum. "Grandma and Aunt Abby want you to bring your friend Krista, too."

"They do?" He glanced at Krista and her startled expression told him she'd heard her name. Kind of hard not to when Shelby was practically shouting into the phone. "OK, I'll ask her, but she might have to work."

"I hope not, but maybe she can switch with someone?" Shelby knew more about hospital shift work than most kids her age, thanks to her mother, who was an ED physician.

"I'll ask," he repeated. "Bye, Shelby." He hung up the phone, glancing at Krista. He cleared his throat.

"I'm sure you heard. You're invited to our family dinner this Sunday. If you're not working?"

"I'm off." She paused, her expression uncertain. Slowly she nodded. "Sure. I'd love to come."

CHAPTER SEVEN

ADAM didn't see much of Krista over the next few days, just the occasional encounter when he made rounds at the hospital. He'd checked on Joy, pleased with her progress. The baby should be ready for discharge in a few days, maybe longer depending on how long it took to place her in a temporary foster-home.

After he'd made rounds, though, he'd had to go back to the clinic. The flu season had hit and he had dozens of sick kids flocking in to seek medical attention. Even though Phoebe was back from her trip, they were so busy he went home late more often than not.

On Friday, as he closed down the clinic later than usual, he thought he saw the same woman as before, the one wearing the dark blue scarf over her head. She was standing down at the bus stop, so he turned up his coat collar against the biting cold wind and headed down to the bus stop to talk to her.

She must have seen him coming because suddenly she was gone. Swearing under his breath, he broke into a run, searching the crowded streets for her. With only two weeks until Christmas, the area was packed with shoppers laden with bags and packages. He dodged people, trying to figure out which way she'd gone, desperate to get at least close enough to take her picture.

Twenty minutes later, he was forced to admit he'd lost her. But even as he stomped toward his car, he knew he was onto something. The scarf woman's guilty actions, the way she'd disappeared to avoid him made him all the more determined to talk to her. She had to be Joy's mother. She just had to be.

He thought of Krista's plan to become a temporary foster-mother to Joy. While admirable, he wondered if she really understood what she was getting herself into. Babies were adorable, no doubt about that, but they were also a huge responsibility. He stomach twisted as he remembered the night he'd lost his son. The pain and agony of watching Danielle double over in pain, knowing she was losing the baby yet helpless to do anything to prevent it.

He never wanted to go through that again. Blocking the images from the past, he took a deep breath and stared through the windshield, waiting for his car to warm up, assailed by doubts. Had he made a mistake in inviting Krista to his parents' for dinner? No matter how hard he tried to convince himself otherwise, he felt as if he was being slowly drawn into something resembling a relationship.

He remembered the kiss they'd shared and was stunned by his intense longing to repeat the experience. Krista deserved someone better, but he hadn't imagined her response to him. His body tightened at the memory.

What would she say if he called her? Would she agree to see him?

He actually took his phone out to dial her number, which she'd given to him the other day as they'd made arrangements for him to pick her up to take her to his parents' for dinner, before he remembered she was working second shift.

Snapping his phone shut, he headed for the hospital. He was crazy, but couldn't seem to stop himself from wanting to see Krista.

Even if it only meant more heartache for him in the end once she knew the truth.

Krista was having a busy night. They had an influx of babies with flu being admitted because of dehydration. After she'd started her third IV, she glanced at the clock, wondering how many more patients they could possibly take on before the end of the shift. There were only two empty beds, but that didn't mean some other patient might be discharged or moved to another floor to make room for more.

Adam walked onto the unit, wearing his black leather coat and looking devastatingly handsome. Her heart slammed against her ribs when his gaze sought and met hers. He carried a large white bag. A hint of peanut oil, soy sauce and ginger tickled her nose and made her mouth water.

"Hi, Krista. Do you have time to take a break for dinner?" He held up the white bag.

"Dinner?" Chinese. There had to be Chinese food in that bag he held. She shook her head with real regret even as her stomach gurgled. "I don't think so, Adam. As much as I'd like to, I don't think I should leave the floor right now. We've been flooded with admissions."

She didn't want anything to happen in her absence, not like the other day when she'd gone to lunch and Britney had arrested.

"Britney is fine, Krista," Adam said, in that annoying way he had of reading her mind. "She tolerated surgery very well and is recovering nicely in PICU."

"I know. But, still, I don't think I should leave."

"What if we stayed up here, in the break room?" Adam persisted. "I brought plenty to share. The rest of the nurses can eat, too."

He was sweet to understand her dilemma. Relieved that he wouldn't press the issue, she nodded. "All right, thanks. Let me just tell Emma and Jenny I'm taking my break now but that I'm nearby if they need me."

She hurried off and talked to both nurses and returned as quickly as possible a few minutes later. Adam had unpacked all the white containers, filling the break room with a tantalizing aroma of ginger.

"You need to eat, Krista," he gently chided as she filled her plate with succulent sweet and sour shrimp over rice. "It's not healthy to skip meals."

Odd comment, coming from him. Danielle's appetite had been anything but robust, one way she had managed to maintain her slim figure. Krista had always eaten when she'd been hungry, which was why she wasn't willowy slim like Danielle. "I'm fine, Adam. Thanks for bringing this over. Much better than the sandwich I slapped together at home in case we were too busy to go down to the cafeteria."

"The clinic has been swamped with patients, too." He helped himself to a plate and took a seat across from her. "Luckily, so far we haven't needed to admit any of our patients."

She had been a tad disappointed when none of her new admissions had been from Adam's clinic.

An awkward silence fell. She glanced at him from beneath her lashes, even as she made quick work of her meal. Why was he here? Because he didn't have anything better to do? Because he felt sorry for her? The thought was depressing.

Just as she was about to ask, Jenny came rushing into the break room. "Krista? Olivia, my new admission in room 604 is throwing up. Can you help me? I'm worried she'll aspirate."

"Of course." Krista sent Adam an apologetic glance. "I'm sorry, but I need to go."

"I understand." He stood, regarding her steadily, "I'll see you tomorrow, Krista. I'll pick you up at six-thirty."

"I'll be ready." Her smile dimmed a bit, thinking about dinner at his parents' house. Shelby's voice had been easy to hear and she suspected he'd only asked her to go because it would have been rude not to. Was he doing all this from some sort of misplaced responsibility? Because she was Danielle's sister and he felt as if he needed to take care of her? "Thanks again for dinner, Adam."

"My pleasure."

Despite her efforts to push Adam from her mind, the deep timbre of his voice stayed with her throughout the rest of her busy shift, filling her with anticipation for what was yet to come.

Krista agonized over what to wear to meet Adam's parents. As she'd been scheduled to work the past three days in a row, she hadn't had time to shop, even if she'd had money to spare, which she didn't.

Difficult decisions, but saving money for a potential upgrade to a two-bedroom apartment for Joy won over clothes for herself, hands down.

Glancing at her watch, she realized the morning was almost over. And she still needed to talk to Mr Baumgartner, the superintendent of her apartment building. She went down to the first floor and knocked on his door, but he didn't answer. Following the sounds of banging, she found the older man in the basement, working on the plumbing leading to the washer and dryer.

"Mr Baumgartner?" She tapped him on the shoulder, knowing from experience he was rather hard of hearing.

"Eh?" He spun around to face her, covering his surprise with a scowl. "What?"

She used her brightest smile. "Do you know if there are any two-bedroom units coming available soon?" Like in the next week? Not likely, but she already had a plan. If a two-bedroom was becoming vacant and she put money down on it, maybe the city social work office would give her the benefit of the doubt and grant her temporary receiving home privileges.

"A two-bedroom unit?" He glared at her from beneath bushy gray eyebrows. With his rather rotund figure, she was struck by the image of him wearing a Santa suit. He'd be an awesome Santa. If he'd lose the perpetual scowl. "Why? You inviting some no-good young man to move in with you?"

She sighed, refusing to point out that if she were actually inviting some young man to move in with her, they'd hardly need a second bedroom—they'd be sharing one. First Adam had jumped to the conclusion some guy had come on to her and now Mr Baumgartner thought she was going to cohabit. Pretty sad to realize everyone assumed she had a better social life than she actually had.

A thought that brought her back full circle to the worry over what she'd wear to meet Adam's parents, her first date in over three months.

Forget about the date. Think about Joy.

"No, Mr Baumgartner, I wouldn't even think of living with a man." The statement was difficult to make while keeping a straight face. "There's an abandoned baby girl at the hospital who needs a place to stay for a short while. I'd like to bring her home with me."

"Oh, yeah?" His eyes narrowed, glancing down at her waist as if checking to see if she was telling the truth or just planning for her own future baby. Good grief, one had to have sex before one could get pregnant. "I heard the Olsons are looking for a house. If they find one, their apartment will be available, but I don't expect that will happen until the spring."

Spring was too far away, but she forced herself to nod. "Good to know. Please, tell me if anything changes, will you? I'd really like to upgrade to a two-bedroom apartment as soon as possible."

"I guess." Mr Baumgartner grunted and turned back to his leaky pipes.

She left him to it, slowly going back upstairs to her place. Trying not to be too depressed by the news, she stood in front of her closet again. She wasted several hours trying on one outfit after another without success. Her dressy clothes seemed too dressy and her casual clothes seemed too casual. Maybe she'd just wear her scrubs and claim she'd just come from work.

In the end she decided on a pair of slimming black slacks and a Christmas-red turtleneck sweater that hugged her curves. She tilted her head, taking in her reflection.

Not half-bad, she thought. Fluffing her hair around her face, she added a touch of make-up to bring out her brown eyes and highlight her high cheekbones, the one feature she shared with her gorgeous sister.

When her doorbell buzzer rang, she gave a start, knocking her hairbrush on the floor. Muttering a curse, she picked it back up and smoothed a hand over her hip.

Willing her heart to settle down, she went to let Adam in.

Adam's mouth went dry when he got a good look at Krista. How in the world had Austin remembered her as being plain? She was beautiful.

Amazingly, send-your-heart-into-asystole beautiful.

"Hi, Adam, come on in." She stepped back, allowing him into the secured area of her apartment building.

The lock didn't look that sturdy, though, he thought with a frown as he followed her to the second floor. Any man intent on getting in wouldn't allow the flimsy lock to stop him.

"Can I get you something to drink?" Krista asked, as she led him into the apartment. He glanced around, not surprised to discover she'd made a home out of practically nothing. The place was decorated to the hilt for Christmas—a wreath on the door, tiny bells dangling from the curtains over her windows, a fairly good-sized tree in the corner of her living room, branches laden with ornaments. Popcorn and cranberry garlands, which he'd bet she'd made herself, encircled the tree.

"No, I'm fine." He slid his hands into his pockets when he saw the mistletoe hanging over her doorway. If he took off his coat and pulled her into his arms, they'd never make it to his parents' house for dinner. He cleared his throat, hoping she didn't pick up on his less-than-honorable thoughts. "My parents are serving hot spiced rum before dinner, if you don't mind heading straight over?"

Her bright smile sent a shaft of desire straight to his groin. Danger, he thought, taking a hasty step back. He didn't trust himself to stay away from her much longer. The need to kiss her was fierce.

"I don't mind at all." She walked to the small closet and drew out her coat.

He took a deep breath, before moving forward to take the long ebony coat from her hands and hold it out for her. The scent of evergreen trees and cranberries weren't just from the tree but clung to her hair. Did she bathe in the stuff? He smoothed the coat over her shoulders and stepped back. "Ready?"

"Yes." They left the close atmosphere of her apartment and headed for his car. He had no idea what they chatted about as he navigated the snow-dusted streets of the city.

"I'm supposed to say thank you," she said, turning toward him in the dim interior of the car.

"Thanks?" He raised a brow. "For what?"

"Dinner last night." She flashed him an odd look. "Chinese food, remember? Jenny, Emily and the rest of the staff really enjoyed your dinner."

"Oh, yeah." He had gone home to his empty condo, tossing and turning for hours before he'd finally fallen asleep. Thank heavens it hadn't been his Saturday to work the clinic. "Tell them they're welcome. It's not a big deal. Nurses bail physicians out all the time."

That made her laugh. "I'm glad you realize it," she said in a teasing tone. "Anyway, it's been totally nuts on the floor the past few nights. We ran back to the break room any time we had five free minutes to eat."

Cold Chinese food? He grimaced. "Glad I could help."

"Tell me who's going to be at your parents' tonight."

Was she nervous about meeting his family? No, she'd grown up in the same area and had gone to high school with several of his siblings. "You know Abby, she'll be there with her husband Nick, but my sister Alaina can't make it tonight. You know my brother Alec, he'll be there with his daughter Shelby and his wife Jillian. My brother Austin is home for the holidays, he'll be there." He slanted her a curious glance, seeking a reaction to Austin's name, but she simply nodded. "You'll like my parents, they're great."

"I'm sure they are."

Damn, he was tempted to kiss her again. He cleared his throat and concentrated on driving. The little bit of snow that had fallen had made the roads slippery.

He parked in front of his parents' house and took Krista's arm to help steady her as they walked up to the door. Even through her bulky coat he could feel heat radiating off her skin. He knocked twice before walking in.

Everyone was already there, the noise level higher than he'd remembered. Krista's eyes widened for a moment but once he drew her forward and began introducing her, she relaxed.

"Mom, Dad, I'd like you to meet Krista Vaughn. Krista, these are my parents, Abe and Alice Monroe."

"It's so nice to meet you." Krista shook hands with both of them.

"Krista, it's good to see you again!" Abby came forward and enveloped her in a welcoming hug. "I'm so glad Adam brought you along. Come on, I want you to meet my husband Nick."

Adam hung back, watching as his family surrounded Krista, making her comfortable without the slightest hesitation. He'd had some reservations about bringing her but, of course, Krista fit right in, just like he'd known she would. His gut clenched when his mother sent him a sly wink of approval.

"Krista, I remember you from high school," Austin said as he moved forward to take her hand. "You're prettier than ever."

"Thank you." Krista's fair skin blushed easily, and Adam sent his brother a warning glance, which Austin cheerfully ignored. Since his younger brother was actually smiling for the first time since he'd been home, Adam let it go.

But if his brother's smile turned into anything more, he was dead meat.

"Something to drink, Krista?" Abe asked in his loud booming voice. "We have hot apple cider or the spiced rum cider, which is my favorite." He winked at her. "Or I can open a bottle of red wine if you'd prefer."

"I'll try the spiced rum cider, since it's your favorite," Krista said.

"Good choice." Abe grinned and Adam knew Krista had won his dad over easily. Although his dad was a pushover for a pretty face. "Adam, will you fetch a few more mugs from the kitchen?"

"Sure." He walked past Krista, lightly brushing her arm as he passed. She shot him a secret smile and in that moment he knew he didn't have to worry about Austin.

Krista was happy to be there with him.

He found the Christmas mugs and carried them back into the living room. Shelby was showing Krista her doctor's bag and explaining how the various instruments worked. He'd heard Shelby mention often enough how much she wanted to be a doctor, but had expected the novelty to have worn off by now. He had to admit, he was surprised it hadn't.

Abby and Nick were talking about the Children's Memorial Christmas ball, where proceeds from the sale of the tickets would go to support medical care for kids in need.

Kids like Joy.

He usually attended, most of the physicians on staff did. He'd planned to go alone as usual but, glancing at Krista, he was struck by the idea of taking her with him.

"She's great, Adam," his mother whispered. "I like her."

He did, too, but he didn't want to raise his mother's hopes. Especially when his mother had strong-armed him into bringing her in the first place. "Take it easy Mom, this is our first date. Try not to start planning a wedding yet, OK?"

"I'll try," she said, but he didn't believe her.

Alec stood and took Jillian's hand. "Listen up, everyone, we have an announcement to make."

Adam stared at his brother, his smile fading.

"Jillian and I are having a baby! Shelby is going to be a big sister." Alec couldn't have looked happier—in fact, he beamed with pride. "Our baby is due some time the end of June."

His family erupted into pandemonium.

Adam stood there, his face frozen. He was truly happy for his brother. For years Alec hadn't known about Shelby but once he'd discovered he had a daughter, he'd instantly changed his bachelor lifestyle to make room for her.

His stomach knotted, wondering how his family would feel if they knew he had once been an expectant father? If they knew his stillborn son had died mere days before Christmas?

The pressure built in his chest until he couldn't stand it. Krista was looking at him with concern, but he ignored her.

"Congrats, Alec. Jillian." He tried to smile but knew he'd failed. Blindly, he turned and walked out of the room, through the kitchen and outside, without his coat, heading straight into the cold winter night.

CHAPTER EIGHT

IF SHE hadn't been sneaking glances at Adam, she might have missed the flash of pain that had darkened his eyes moments before he spun on his heel and disappeared into the kitchen. When she heard a door open and close, she hurried after him.

"Adam?" She opened the kitchen door, peering through the snow flurries to find him. With help from a streetlight on the corner, she could just make out the dark shadow of his broad-shouldered frame striding down the driveway. He didn't respond when she called his name so she followed him, shivering as the chilly wind cut through her cotton turtleneck sweater.

He wasn't wearing a coat, and she didn't want to lose him by taking the time to find hers.

What had happened? Why did Adam seem so upset about his brother's announcement? Maybe it wasn't Alec's news that had bothered Adam, but something certainly had.

For the life of her, she couldn't figure out what.

"Adam!" She broke into a run, her feet slipping a little on the snow-covered sidewalk. At least picking up her pace helped keep her blood flowing. It was freezing out here, she really should have grabbed her coat. "Wait up."

He turned to see her dashing toward him and stopped. Then he retraced his steps to meet her. He caught her close in a hug but the way he rubbed his hands over her arms and back told her he was only trying to keep her warm. "Are you crazy? You shouldn't be out here without a coat."

She refrained from pointing out the obvious, that he wasn't wearing one either. She clenched her jaw to prevent her teeth from chattering. "Adam, what's wrong? Why are you out here?"

He wrapped an arm around her shoulders and headed back up towards the house. "Come on, we need to get you inside before you get sick."

She didn't argue, even though he hadn't answered her question. And she ignored the tiny flash of hurt caused by his unwillingness to confide in her. Once again he was shutting her out, refusing to talk about his emotions. He'd done the same thing after Devon's transfer to PICU, but this was worse. After they mounted the steps to the back porch she paused, looking up at him. "Are you sure you're all right, Adam? Would you rather leave?"

"I'm fine." His smile was strained. "I just needed a moment alone. My mother would freak out if we left before dinner. Besides, I'm hungry."

He opened the door for her and she stepped into the warmth of the Monroe family kitchen with a tiny sigh of relief. Glistening snowflakes dotted Adam's dark hair and she wished again he'd confide in her, explain what was going on beneath that calm façade of his.

Luckily none of the Monroes seemed to have noticed their brief disappearance outside, or, if they had, they didn't mention it as the family prepared to sit down for dinner. Alice brought mountains of food to the table, two hearty pot roasts with gravy, a couple of green bean casseroles and a huge bowl of small red potatoes. Somehow she wasn't surprised to discover Alice had made warm apple cobbler for dessert.

Krista subtly tugged at the snug waistband of her black slacks, thinking it was a good thing she didn't eat like this every day or she'd grow out of her clothes very quickly.

"So how is baby Joy, Adam?" Abby asked, sneaking a bite of cobbler from her husband's plate. "Is she still in the hospital?"

"Yeah." Adam nodded, glancing over at Krista. "She's doing really well, and I think she'll be ready for discharge in a few days."

"Baby Joy?" Austin echoed, a puzzled frown furrowed his brow. "One of your patients?"

"An abandoned baby," Alec explained. "Left in Adam's clinic."

"She was sick, but Krista helped nurse her back to good health," Adam said. "She had a viral infection, but she's recovered well."

"Growing like a weed," Krista added.

"The poor thing," Alice murmured, her expression troubled. "I hope things work out for her."

When Alice stood to begin clearing dishes, Krista rose to her feet to help. Abby did, too, and shot meaningful glances at her brothers. "Mom, sit down. We'll take care of the dishes." Austin and Adam exchanged knowing looks, both rising to their feet to pitch in.

"Nonsense." Alice ignored her daughter until Adam grabbed the stack of dirty dishes right from her hands.

"It's no use, Mom. Why make us go through the same argument every time?" Adam wasn't taking no for an answer. "We'll take care of it. Go sit down with Dad."

With a sigh, Alice sat. Most of the Monroe siblings jumped up to help, but the kitchen really wasn't large enough for everyone to fit, so somehow Krista and Austin ended up together, manning the sink to wash and dry dishes while the rest of the clan cleared the table and put the leftovers away.

"Nick bought us tickets for the Christmas ball. Is anyone else going?" Abby wanted to know.

"What Christmas ball?" Austin asked, his hands immersed in a sink full of soapy water.

"It's a charity for Children's Memorial Hospital," Krista told him. "They always hold it the weekend before Christmas."

"Really? Sounds like fun." Austin nudged her with his elbow. Was he suggesting they should go together? "Krista, I'd love to see you wearing a pretty ballgown."

She raised a brow at his comment. "Austin, are you flirting with me?"

Austin winked, reminding her of his and Adam's father. It was obvious where the Monroe men had gotten their charm. Abe Monroe was a flatterer, too.

"He'd better not be," Adam said in a low voice, setting a stack of dirty dishes next to his brother. He gave him a playful punch in the shoulder. "Not good form to move in on my date, bro."

"Hey, I was just making innocent conversation," Austin protested.

"Innocent?" Adam muttered under his breath as he walked back into the dining room.

Austin flashed a secret smile. "See? It's working. I bet he'll ask you to go."

She rolled her eyes, returning his smile. "Thanks, but I don't think I need your help." She'd rather Adam asked her to the ball because he really wanted to go with her, not because of some silly, adolescent competition with his brother. The fact he'd only invited her tonight because his family had pushed the issue was bad enough.

Cleaning up the mess from the meal didn't take long, with everyone's help. And shortly afterwards people started to say their goodbyes.

On the way home, Krista sat back, humbled at how Adam's parents and siblings had welcomed her into the fold. "You have a wonderful family, Adam."

"Yeah, I know." He paused, concentrating on the road for a bit before asking, "Speaking of family, how's your Aunt Bea doing?"

Krista glanced at him, surprised he'd remembered the one family member she'd truly liked. Her smile was sad. "Actually, she passed away a few months ago."

Adam winced. "I'm sorry, Krista. I know you two were close."

"Thanks." She shrugged, striving for a light tone. "She died peacefully in her sleep, so I can't complain. She wasn't nearly as mobile as she wanted to be after her stroke."

Obviously, he remembered that night he'd helped her with Aunt Bea. First he'd rescued her from her date, then had taken charge with Aunt Bea's illness. He'd always been her knight, riding to the rescue, but she wasn't satisfied with that any longer.

She wanted a partner, a man to raise a family with. Glancing at his closed expression, she couldn't make herself believe Adam was that man.

He pulled up in front of her apartment complex and kept the engine running as he reached over to take her hand. "You're welcome to come to our house for the holiday. My family would love to have you."

His family? Not him personally? The offer was sweet, but she sensed he was feeling sorry for her because, like Joy, she didn't have any family left. Or rather, she had family but didn't much care for them, as her aunts and uncles had made her and Danielle's lives miserable. She did have her sister, but Danielle lived practically on the other side of the world. For all practical purposes, she was alone. Like Joy. The thought was depressing. "Thanks, but I'm working the holiday."

"I understand." He frowned a bit and turned off the car. "I'll walk you up to the door."

An awkward silence fell between them as he accompanied her to the door. She briefly toyed with the idea of asking him in, but thought he'd refuse as they both had to work the next day.

At the door, he leaned down and brushed his mouth against hers in a light, friendly kiss. She fought down the urge to throw herself into his arms. "Goodnight, Krista."

"Goodnight, Adam. Thanks for the lovely dinner." Forcing herself to turn away, she unlocked the door and went inside.

Sleep didn't come easily. She kept thinking that

somehow, even though Adam had been kind enough to invite her to meet his family, they'd ended up back on friendship terms. It was almost as if that heated kiss they'd shared at the hospital had never happened.

Other than that brief moment when he'd seemed jealous of Austin's harmless flirting, Adam had treated her as a lonely waif his family needed to adopt rather than a woman he was attracted to.

On Monday Krista returned to work, dismayed to discover that Joy had taken a turn for the worse. "She's been throwing up for the past couple of hours," Emma informed her during report. "I'm afraid she's come down with flu."

"We've had more than a few flu patients here," Krista agreed. "I guess we shouldn't be surprised."

"I got an order from Dr Monroe to start an IV. Do you have time to put it in?" Emma asked, giving a harried glance around the nurses' station. "I still need to give report to Helen, too. Jamie Raasch, my other patient, has also spiked a fever and we need to get blood cultures on her."

"Sure." Krista gathered together the supplies she'd need to start the IV and headed into Joy's room. The baby was staring up at the mobile Krista had strung up for her. Joy seemed too listless, compared to how well she'd been doing the last time she'd worked.

"Oh, sweetheart," she murmured, picking the baby up and cradling her against her shoulder. "You'll feel better soon, I promise."

She carried Joy over to the procedure table and strapped her in. Joy's pathetic cries stabbed her heart and she did her best to ignore the wailing sound as she looked for the best vein to use as a site for the IV.

When she found a decent scalp vein, she prepped the skin with antiseptic solution and then used some topical lidocaine jelly on the area so that the needle poke would hurt less. She waited the required time for the medication to work, then picked up the tiny catheter. Her stomach tightened painfully and her fingers shook as she held the bevel of the needle over the skin.

For a long moment she stared down at Joy, feeling sick to her stomach as a thin bead of sweat trickled down her back.

She couldn't do it.

Even knowing she'd used the numbing medicine to prevent the needle stick from hurting too badly, she still couldn't do it. Using one hand to slip the cap back over the needle to keep it sterile, she took a step back, watching Joy as she cried from within the confines of her restraints. Dear heavens, what was wrong with her? She'd started numerous IVs in babies—why was this suddenly so different?

She took a deep breath and let it out in a whoosh. Joy needed IV fluids, already she could see the early signs of dehydration. Babies didn't have a lot of body weight so they were prone to become dehydrated much faster than adults would. Steeling her resolve, she stepped up to the procedure table again, trying to look at Joy as just another patient rather than the baby girl she'd fallen in love with.

"Krista?" Adam's voice startled her and she swung around to find him standing in the doorway. His expression held concern as his gaze met hers. "Are you all right?"

How long had he been there? she wondered. Guilt intermixed with embarrassment washed over her. "I just…can't seem to get this IV started."

"Do you want me to do it?" Adam stepped further into the room.

She knew she was being a complete coward, but nodded and waited until he'd donned a pair of gloves before carefully handing him the catheter. "I'd appreciate it."

She could hardly watch, biting her lip as Joy's cries increased in volume, despite the numbing medicine. She held Joy's feet as Adam threaded the needle into her scalp vein. Once he had it secure, she held up the end of the IV tubing so he could connect it to the catheter, relieved the procedure was over.

"Thanks, Adam."

"No problem." He stepped back and allowed her to unbuckle the baby from the procedure table. "You looked pale for a few minutes there. Are you feeling all right? You're not coming down with flu, too, I hope."

"No, I don't feel sick." At least, not any more, now that the IV was safely in. She held Joy against her chest, an overwhelming feeling of love and caring sweeping over her.

She needed to transfer Joy's care to another nurse. There was no reason she shouldn't have been able to place the IV, other than her inability to see Joy as a patient. She glanced at Adam, hoping he hadn't noticed. "So far she's thrown up twice, from what Emma told me in report."

Adam nodded. "I came over to check on her, before seeing the rest of my patients. If anything changes, give me a call. I should be here at the hospital for at least another hour or so."

"I will." She waited until he had left, before sitting down in the rocker, stealing a few minutes to cuddle Joy close. The baby smelled sweet, innocent. The thought of handing Joy over to some stranger ripped a hole in her heart.

What if her application to be a temporary carer was denied? She wanted the baby to be loved and cared for, not sent into the system to be a responsibility for some overworked foster-family.

Maybe she should be hoping and praying the baby's mother returned. Being with her real mother had to be better than the foster system, right? She swallowed hard and pressed a kiss to the top of Joy's soft head. In the time Joy had been there, the baby girl had taken up residence in her heart.

After switching patient assignments with another nurse, she sought and found Shirley, the unit social worker. "Shirley? I haven't heard anything regarding the status of my application yet."

"I'm not surprised." Shirley gave an apologetic shrug. "The wheels of bureaucracy turn slow, Krista. You know it takes a good six weeks to get through the entire process. At least you had a head start. They're always looking for good foster-parents. I'm sure you'll hear from them soon. Probably some time after the holiday."

"I hope so." Krista forced a smile, hoping Shirley wasn't just saying that to make her feel better. "I'd really like Joy to live with me. I even have a potential babysitter lined up, in case everything works out." Mrs Granger, one of the widows in the apartment building, had agreed to babysit for Joy. The only problem was the lack of a two-bedroom apartment, something she hoped the department of health and human services wouldn't hold against her.

"Sounds like you have everything planned out." Shirley smiled. "Hang in there, I'm sure they'll be in touch soon."

"I will." Krista turned away, wishing she felt as confident. She made rounds, checking on all her patients, and gave Jeffrey McNally the IV antibiotic he was scheduled to receive.

Once the antibiotic had infused, she disconnected the toddler's IV and lifted him into her arms, grunting a bit beneath his weight. Next to Joy, the eighteen-month-old toddler felt as heavy as a concrete brick.

She took him into the nurses' station to put him in the swing so she could keep an eye on him. After a few minutes, though, she wrinkled her nose, realizing his diaper needed to be changed. With a sigh she took him back out of the swing.

"Krista?" Adam came down the hall toward her. He frowned a little and stood with his hands in his pockets. "According to the patient assignment board, you're not the nurse taking care of Joy any more."

"No." Krista's smile was wan. "I guess you were right. I've grown too attached to her. When it came time to put that IV in, I couldn't do it." She shifted Jeffrey on her hip, disliking the way Adam had observed her failure. "I'm going to keep visiting her as often as I can, though."

"I see." He fell in step with her as she headed down the hall, back to Jeffrey's room. "I have to leave, but wanted to ask you a question first."

She lifted a brow, wondering what he wanted. Something about Joy? Did he want her to stay away from the baby? Hesitant, she asked, "What?"

"Will you come with me to the Christmas ball this Friday night?"

Flabbergasted, she stopped and stared at him. She'd never expected this. Had he asked her because of Austin's meddling? She hoped not. Her emotions were already too involved with Adam, heck, with his entire family. It would be better for her to refuse, to put some needed distance between them. She was fairly certain he didn't return her feelings. In fact, she suspected more than anything he felt sorry for her.

The last thing she wanted or needed from Adam was pity.

She opened her mouth, willing herself to be strong, but heard herself agree. "Yes. I'd love to."

"Great." Adam's warm grin rocked her on her heels. "I'll pick you up at seven."

"I'll be ready." So much for protecting her heart, she thought as she watched him walk away. Absently untangling Jeffrey's grip on her hair, she realized maybe she was wrong about Adam seeing her only as a friend.

The expression in his gaze when she'd agreed to go to the ball with him had reminded her of the moment they'd kissed, full of suppressed heat and anticipation. Her lips tingled at the memory.

Maybe going to the ball together would prove to be the changing point in their relationship. A chance for Adam to see her as a desirable woman rather than a family-less waif.

A smile tugged at the corner of her mouth.

With determined resolve she decided to use every feminine weapon at her disposal to make it happen. She'd grown a lot during this past year—certainly she had the self-confidence to do this.

If Adam still didn't notice her as a woman, it wouldn't be for lack of trying on her part.

CHAPTER NINE

ADAM knew he was totally losing his mind when he used what limited free time he had to stand at the bus stop located a few blocks from his clinic. He wasn't going to finish his Christmas shopping this way, he thought, hanging out in the doorway of a discount drug store and stomping his feet to stimulate circulation in his toes.

He felt ridiculous, especially as the sidewalks remained pretty crowded with the Christmas shopping rush. People passed him by in a whirl of motion, it was hard to watch every individual. He could be freezing his feet off for no reason.

There she was! He straightened, his gaze zeroing in on the woman who stood directly under the bus-stop sign. Where had she come from? Did she work somewhere nearby that she always used this bus stop? Or did she keep coming back just to peer through the doorway into his clinic?

Keeping his hat low on his forehead so she wouldn't recognize him and run, he shifted his position until he stood in a spot where he could see her better. Keeping his head down as much as possible, he lifted his phone until he could see her clearly and snapped a picture of her. From what he could tell, she was younger than he'd originally estimated, in her mid- to late twenties. He could only see her profile but was willing to take what he could get. He took several photos, hoping for at least one decent shot that Alec could use to help discover her identity. The screen on his phone was small and it was dark outside, but when he was satisfied he'd captured her image, he took several steps back, trying to think of the best way to approach her.

A bus pulled up. He lost his chance. She didn't notice him but stood in line to get on the bus so, instead of calling out to her, he followed the crowd, mounting the steps until he was on the bus too. He hadn't ridden the bus since his college days, but passed her with his gaze averted until he was several rows behind her before taking his seat. As the bus pulled away from the curb, he sat back, hoping he could maybe at least find out where the scarf woman lived.

He didn't like feeling like a stalker. Hurting her was the last thing on his mind but, heaven knew, she'd have no way of knowing his intentions were honorable. Slouching down in his seat, he debated calling Alec. As a cop, Alec could probably talk to her without causing too much alarm.

He dialed his brother's number and held his breath, waiting for him to answer. When the ringing stopped and Alec's voicemail message came on, he spoke, keeping his voice low. "Alec? Call me. I have information on our project."

Snapping his phone shut, he watched the scarf woman. She didn't interact with anyone, but held onto her purse in her lap and stared straight ahead, not encouraging any conversation. Unlike many of the bus patrons, she didn't wear headphones to listen to music or read.

They rode for at least thirty minutes before she reached up to grab the pull cord, indicating her desire to get off. Adam peered through the window. Did she live nearby? He made note of the street names on the corner, committing them to memory. The scarf woman disembarked from the bus, but he didn't immediately follow.

He waited until the next bus stop to get off. The wind was cold but it wasn't snowing as he walked down the street back toward the corner where the woman had gotten off.

The neighborhood was far from wealthy, but it wasn't too bad. Quite honestly, he'd almost expected something worse, considering she must have been desperate to have given up her baby. Did she have other children? Did she live alone? Or was she living in some sort of abusive relationship?

He knew he was letting his imagination run amok, but he couldn't seem to stop filtering through the various possibilities. Trying to convince himself that simply talking to the woman wouldn't do any harm, even if she was in some sort of precarious situation, he hunched his shoulders and crossed the street. Once Alec had a name to go with the face, they'd know more about her background. If something was wrong, they'd likely find out from her police record, if she had one. He refused to do anything that might cause her more trouble in the long run.

It was too far to walk back to his clinic, so he waited for the next bus in order to return to the spot where he'd left his car.

He'd send the pictures and the street names to Alec. Maybe with this additional information they'd be one step closer to finding the identity of the mystery woman and hopefully reuniting Joy with her mother.

On Friday night, he drove to Krista's apartment. He'd sent the pictures of his mystery woman to Alec and already his brother had several street cops asking around the area to see if anyone recognized her. Adam was satisfied they were making progress. He was hopeful they were very close to finding Joy's mother.

Of course, there was the slim possibility his scarf woman wasn't really Joy's mother, but his instincts told him otherwise. And he was definitely a man who followed his gut feelings.

Like asking Krista to the Christmas ball. After he'd come into Joy's room, to see her staring at Joy with the IV catheter in her fingers, he'd known she hadn't been able do the procedure, even before her stricken gaze had met his. He'd warned her about getting too attached to Joy. He understood, though, the baby's innocence definitely had a way of getting into your heart.

It was less than a week before Christmas and the baby would be medically cleared for discharge soon. Joy coming down with the flu was sort of a blessing in disguise—it meant she could legitimately stay in hospital another few days.

And if they didn't have her mother's identity by then, he'd have no choice but to put her into a temporary receiving home. Certainly Joy wouldn't suffer as a result of a few days in a stranger's care. He was convinced Alec would find Joy's mother and with his help the woman would realize there were resources available. Surely the fact that the woman had come to his clinic, as if hoping to see the baby, showed how much she still cared?

He pushed the doubts from his mind, straightened his shoulders and headed inside Krista's apartment block. In the locked landing, he pushed the buzzer for Krista's apartment. Instead of releasing the lock and inviting him up, she told him she'd be right down.

She didn't keep him waiting. Through the glass window he could see her as she walked down the stairs. He sucked in a quick breath at the sight of Krista wearing a fire-engine red strapless dress that hugged every generous curve. His mouth went dry as she met his gaze.

Boy, oh, boy, was he in trouble tonight.

She stepped through the doorway. Belatedly he noticed she held her long wool coat over her arm. "Here." He took the coat from her and held it out. Somehow he managed to find his voice. "You're absolutely beautiful, Krista."

"Thank you." She pulled the edges of her coat together and preceded him to the car. He had to wrestle himself under control, far too tempted to skip the stupid ball altogether, kidnapping her instead and taking her to his condo for a nice quiet evening alone.

He kept the conversation light with an effort, although every nerve in his body was attuned to her presence. Her Christmassy scent, pine trees and cranberries, was driving him crazy. "How was your day?"

"Good. Joy's doing a little better," she said. "I checked on her this morning."

He sent a questioning glance. "On your day off?"

She flushed and nodded. "Yes. I went in to sit with

her for a little while. It's so hard, knowing there isn't anyone in the world who seems to care about her. She's so young, so innocent. She deserves to have a family."

"I know." He reached over, snaring her hand in his. "You care, Krista, and so do many others at the hospital. Remember that Joy isn't ever completely alone. We're going to work together to take care of her."

She nodded and he was glad she didn't pull her hand from his. Krista was going to take it hard when Joy was finally discharged. He pulled up in front of the conference center located in downtown Milwaukee, close to the lakefront, and handed the keys to the parking attendant. Cupping Krista's elbow in his hand, he escorted her inside.

Many of the faculty physicians from Children's Memorial were there, and he greeted several of them, introducing Krista as he went. Many of the men sent her admiring glances and he found himself wishing she hadn't worn such a provocative dress.

He frowned. Had she already had the dress or had she bought it just recently? A stab of guilt hit hard. Damn, he hadn't even thought about that detail when he'd asked her to go with him. He knew Krista didn't have lots of money and Abby was close enough to her size that she could have lent Krista a dress if necessary.

A few of the physicians greeted Krista by name. He kept his hand in the small of her back, knowing he was acting possessively but unable to help himself. He stayed close, even as they went up to help themselves to the appetizers. There was enough food to feed an army, so they ate and drank red wine until the band began to play.

Perfect, a slow song, just what he'd been waiting for. He set down his glass and gently lifted Krista's from her fingers.

"Will you dance with me?" he asked.

She smiled and nodded, holding out her hand.

He led her onto the dance floor and drew her into his arms. His heart swelled and his groin tightened as she pressed against him. He didn't even care when the band played a Christmas tune, he was too happy to be holding Krista in his arms.

Her skin was satiny soft as he trailed his fingers over her bare shoulder. Everyone around them disappeared. All he could see, smell and touch was Krista. She looked like a delectable Christmas present he was dying to unwrap. He willed himself to stay in control, but knew he was in trouble because Krista fit his embrace perfectly. He fought the desperate need to kiss her, and lost.

"Krista," he murmured, before capturing her mouth with his. He wanted to keep the kiss light, gentle, but the moment his mouth touched hers, she opened for him, drawing him into her moist depths, returning his kiss with an enthusiasm that made him groan.

Oblivious to their surroundings, he crushed her close. He suspected his feet had stopped moving, giving up the pretense of dancing, but couldn't bring himself to care. Her mouth was luscious, velvety soft and tasted of promises to come.

"Hey, Adam." Abby and Nick shamelessly bumped into him from behind. "Oh, excuse me, did we interrupt?"

He broke off the kiss, breathing heavily, sending his sister a lethal glare over the top of Krista's head. "Yeah. Get lost."

Nick smirked. "Hey, buddy, you might want to remember you're in a public place. The heat you guys are generating is enough to radiate through the walls and melt the foot of snow covering the ground outside."

Adam suspected his brother-in-law had figured out how close he was to losing it and he did his best to ignore the harsh edge of his need. A couple of amused glances from other couples on the dance floor confirmed that Nick hadn't been the only one to notice. Adam drew in a deep breath, wondering how many numbers he'd missed. From what he could tell, he'd been kissing Krista for ever.

He wanted to keep on kissing her for ever.

It took a few moments for Nick's words to sink in. "Foot of snow on the ground? Since when?"

"Since we got here." His sister's knowing grin set his teeth on edge. You'd think a guy could escape from his family for one night. "Actually, it's not quite a foot deep yet, but will be soon. Didn't you hear the news? They're predicting at least fourteen inches of snow."

"Fourteen inches? That's almost a blizzard." Krista's eyes widened in alarm. "Good grief, I had no idea. I guess I didn't bother listening to the news."

Neither had he. He'd kept the radio off most of the time to avoid the non-stop Christmas music that had the effect of raking fingernails over every one of his exposed nerves.

"Maybe we'd better go," he said, glancing down at Krista. "Before the worst of the storm hits."

"We figured we'd leave early too," Abby confided. "One more dance?" she asked, gazing up at Nick.

"Of course." Nick cuddled her close as they moved away.

Adam didn't trust himself for one more dance, Krista

went to his head faster than any drug. Keeping a tight rein on his hormones, he took Krista's hand and walked back toward the buffet tables. "If you're hungry, let's finish eating before we go."

"Sounds good." She filled another plate, seemingly enjoying herself.

He switched to water, figuring the streets outside would be bad enough without adding the effects of another glass of wine. They took some time to finish eating, and then said their goodbyes as they made their way to the door.

Snowflakes filled the air, the wind whipping them around in a frenzy. By the looks of the dense white flakes, the blizzard had already started. The streets didn't look too bad, though, and when a large snowplow trundled past, he gave the parking attendant his ticket. When his car arrived, he helped Krista inside and then began the long, tortuous ride home.

He kept his speed under twenty-five miles per hour. The streets were slick and visibility was almost non-existent. Twice he almost suggested turning around and going back to find a hotel to spend the night. Only the fact that they were already halfway to Krista's apartment convinced him it would be better to keep going. If his condo had been closer, instead of farther away, he would have gone there.

The traffic lights up ahead turned yellow, then red. He stepped gently on the brake, but the car didn't stop. Instead, it slid sideways, hydroplaning on the ice. Krista gasped and clung to the dashboard as he fought to keep the car on the road.

"Adam?" she gasped as the car kept moving. He wrestled with the steering-wheel but it was useless, he had absolutely no control. The car hit the curb and, along with his foot on the brake, it was enough to bring the car to a stop.

For a long second he stared through the windshield.

If he'd been going any faster, he might have gone up and over the curb, hitting the brick building of the veterinary clinic.

"A little slippery out here." Krista unclamped her fingers from around the doorhandle.

"Yeah. Slippery." Visions of the car accident that had cost him his son's life flashed in his mind. Muttering a curse under his breath, he glanced at her, his gaze apologetic. "Are you all right?"

She nodded. "You weren't going very fast, thank heavens."

Logically he knew the icy road wasn't his fault but he didn't say anything as he shifted into reverse and carefully backed away from the curb. He shifted again and headed back down the street.

This time he crawled at a snail's pace, gripping the steering-wheel so tightly his biceps ached with the effort. It took him another fifteen minutes to get to Krista's apartment. He'd never been so happy to see a building in his life.

For a long moment they just sat there. Then Krista reached for the doorhandle. "You'd better come in." Her expression was serious in the dim light of the car. "There's no way you're driving home in this weather tonight."

He realized she was right. Her suggestion was

logical. Practical. His body had no business reacting as if it was something more. His mind imagined the single-bedroom apartment she lived in and told himself not to read anything into her invitation. No doubt she expected him to sleep on the couch.

"Are you sure?" He considered his options. "There's a hotel not far from here I can probably get to, no problem."

She shook her head, meeting his gaze. "No hotel. I think you should spend the night with me."

CHAPTER TEN

SPEND the night with me. Krista's heart pinged against her ribs like a pinball as she led the way into her apartment building. She couldn't believe she'd been so bold as to say the words out loud. The idea of spending the night with Adam was thrilling and yet scary at the same time. Scary because she hadn't been with a man in a really long time. Her feelings of self-confidence wavered. As she used her key to open the door, Adam reached over her shoulder, enveloping her within the protected circle of his musky scent.

She breathed deep, wanting him. Those moments on the dance floor had filled her with an edgy desire. A feeling she'd never before experienced in the arms of anyone else. They headed upstairs to her apartment just as Mr Baumgartner came down.

"Hi, Mr Baumgartner," she greeted the elderly caretaker.

"Hrmph." The old man scowled at them, and from the way he raked his gaze over Adam, she knew his keen gaze didn't miss a thing. She flushed at the barely veiled accusation in his gaze. For heaven's sake, it wasn't as if she entertained men in her apartment on a regular basis, and even if she did, her private life was none of the caretaker's business. "Don't forget to shovel the sidewalk in the morning," he said in a curt tone as she walked by.

"Don't worry, I won't." She went straight to her apartment door and opened it, glancing back to find Mr Baumgartner still staring after her. She ushered Adam inside and closed the door with a feeling of relief. "Whew. For a minute there I thought he was going to kick you out."

"You shovel the sidewalk for him?" Adam asked with a frown.

"Yeah, he's too old to do it and he knocks fifty bucks a month off my rent in the winter." She shrugged out of her coat and hung it in the tiny closet. Glancing over her shoulder, she watched Adam take his coat off. "Don't you think he'd make a great Santa? At least, he would if we could get him to smile."

Adam came up beside her, hanging his own coat in the closet next to hers. The action implied an intimacy she longed for. Irrationally nervous, she stepped back, trying to think of how to proceed from there. She had him in her apartment, but her seduction skills were pretty rusty. How on earth did she get him from the polite chit-chat phase to the let's-take-off-our-clothes-and-get-naked phase?

"Would you like something to drink?" She walked into the kitchen. "Coffee? Or something stronger?"

"Coffee is fine." Adam's expression remained thoughtful as he took a seat on her sofa. Because her apartment wasn't very big, she could easily see him from the kitchen area. Filling the carafe with water, she filled the coffee-filter and pushed the button.

"What's wrong?" she asked, coming over to sit beside him. "You're not really worried about what Mr Baumgartner thinks, are you?"

"Not exactly." Adam's grin was rueful. "Although he obviously watches out for you in his own weird way, which makes me feel a little better. The security in this place isn't too impressive."

She lifted a brow. "Maybe not, but I'm not helpless. I can take care of myself." There he was again, treating her as if she were a younger sister he was bound by duty to protect.

"I'm surprised you haven't adopted him as a surrogate father." Adam's green gaze carried a hint of compassion. "Considering how you lost your parents so young."

His astuteness surprised her, because she was rather attached to the elderly man, despite his curmudgeonly attitude. "Growing up the way we did, being shuffled from one family to the other, was hard, but it did make me appreciate the value of family." She stood and walked back into the kitchen for the coffee. "And I happen to know Mr Baumgartner lost his wife a few years ago, he had one son who he also lost. He doesn't have any family left. So, yes, I do see him as sort of a surrogate father."

After filling two mugs, she carried a small tray containing cream and sugar and set it on the table within reach.

"Thanks," he murmured, picking up one of the mugs and taking a sip. "Is that why you're so attached to Joy? Because she's all alone in the world, too?"

"I guess so." Staring down at her mug, she wondered how they'd gotten off on such a serious subject. "Most of my life I've felt like the odd person out. I was so different from Danielle, it seemed as if, no matter what I did, I didn't belong." She lifted a shoulder and raised her gaze to his. "I love Joy. If her mother comes back, that's fine, but if not, I intend to be there for her. I want her to feel wanted. Safe and secure in the knowledge that she belongs."

"I know, Krista." He reached over to take her hand in his. "But you must realize single parenthood isn't easy. I watched Alec struggle to adjust to being a single dad, once he learned about his daughter, Shelby. The family chipped in to help, but he had to jockey around his work schedule, going to the graveyard shift just so he could spend more time with his daughter. And he paid a college girl to spend the nights with Shelby while he was working. I can only imagine how much harder it would be with a brand-new baby."

Logically, she knew he was probably right. Being a single parent wouldn't be easy. Yet she felt compelled to take care of Joy, to love the little girl as her own. Of course, life would be perfect if she, Joy and Adam were together, as a family. Only Adam didn't give any indication he felt the same way. "I bet your brother feels as if the sacrifices were well worth the effort."

"I'm sure he does." Adam let go of her hand to pick up his coffee-mug. "But Shelby is his flesh-and-blood daughter."

A spark of anger burst free. "Are you saying I'd love Joy more if she were my own daughter?"

"No." He hastily backpedaled. "Of course not."

"Because my relatives, my own flesh and blood, didn't love me enough to take me and Danielle into their homes," she continued, on a roll. "Much less into their hearts."

"Their loss, Krista," he pointed out softly.

Just that quickly, her anger deflated. "You're right. The loss was theirs."

"I want the same thing for Joy that you do," Adam said in a low tone. "A loving family."

She believed him. He set down his empty mug and patted the sofa cushions.

"Thanks for the coffee and for letting me sleep on your sofa tonight, Krista."

The sofa? Dismay mingled with regret. Why not her bed? Those magical moments on the dance floor seemed a lifetime ago, rather than mere hours. She forced a smile. "I don't mind. It wouldn't have been too smart to drive home in the blizzard."

"I know."

She felt his gaze upon her as she stood, picked up the tray and carried it into the kitchen. Did he sense she wanted more? She squeezed her eyes shut and rubbed the center of her forehead. If only she was better at this whole seduction routine. She hadn't imagined the heat between them on the dance floor—heck, even Abby and Nick had said something. What she wouldn't give to be dancing with Adam again now.

But she'd told him about her past, about her feelings for Joy and wanting a family, and the mood had changed. Maybe his feelings weren't as involved as she'd thought.

Straightening her shoulders, she went back out to the living room. Her step slowed when she discovered Adam had taken off his tuxedo jacket, tie and shoes and was stretched out full length on her sofa, his arm tucked under his head.

He really did plan to sleep.

Hiding the stark disappointment, she went to her room, pulled out a spare pillow and blanket and carried them through to Adam. "Please, make yourself comfortable."

"Thanks, Krista." His murmured response sent a shiver of awareness skating down her back.

"You're welcome." For a moment she hesitated, wanting to bluntly ask him to join her but unable to muster the courage. She turned away heading down the hall to her room. "Goodnight, Adam."

"Goodnight."

For a long time she stared at the ceiling above her head, hating how she'd taken the coward's way out. Torn between wanting to offer herself to Adam and fear of rejection, she was annoyed to realize she still hadn't quite overcome her youthful feelings of inadequacy.

Adam didn't get a whole lot of sleep on Krista's sofa, and while he would have liked to blame the narrow, short frame, he knew the real reason was because her pillow and blankets smelled like her.

Reminding him throughout the whole night that she slept just a few feet down the hall. Wearing something soft, clingy, or maybe even nothing at all. Oh, yeah, his imagination could easily picture her wearing nothing but her beautiful ivory skin.

He wanted her. In the bright light of the morning he sat up and scrubbed his hands over his face. The hard ache in his groin had kept him on edge all night, but he'd ignored the need, knowing it wasn't fair to take advantage of the situation. His body was more than willing to take his relationship with Krista to the next level, but emotionally he wasn't as sure.

He couldn't take things to the next step until he'd told her the truth about the car accident and losing his son. For a moment last night he'd almost told her, had been tempted to blurt out the truth, but had held back. First, because dancing with her at the ball had been so magical he hadn't wanted to ruin the evening. Second, he realized he'd gotten so used to hiding his feelings he wasn't sure how to change.

And there was always the possibility Krista would be horrified once she learned the truth.

His fault. If he hadn't been arguing with Danielle that night, he would have seen the truck barreling through the intersection straight toward them. There had been time to avoid the accident. Plenty of time to save his son.

That night still haunted him. In the hospital, the nurses had wrapped his stillborn son and asked if he wanted to hold him. He'd taken his son, stared down at his tiny, perfect face and knew he'd failed him.

Danielle had been crying, refusing to see or hold the baby.

He knew he needed to put the past to rest. Nothing would bring his son back. But he couldn't let go of his guilt. Couldn't even bring himself to talk about it. All these months the burden of his loss was enough to keep him celibate.

Until now. Krista tempted him as he'd never been

tempted before. The more time he spent with her, the more he liked her.

The more he wanted her.

She was so brave, the way she'd told him about her past. He really did understand her need for family. He'd almost taken her into his arms to comfort her, but hadn't trusted himself to stop at simple comfort. Not when he'd wanted so much more.

He'd promised himself he wouldn't take advantage of the snowstorm. Painful or not, he'd kept his promise.

With a muttered groan, he stood and padded to the kitchen to start a pot of coffee. Outside the snow had finally stopped and he suspected Krista would be soon heading outside to shovel snow off the sidewalk outside the apartment building.

No way was he going to let her do the chore all alone.

"Good morning," she greeted him, coming into the kitchen. She was dressed for work in snug jeans and a cream-colored cable-knit sweater. "Are you hungry? I have pancake mix."

"Sure." He was more interested in making sure she ate something, so he helped her prepare breakfast, enjoying the coziness of her apartment as they ate pancakes sprinkled with chocolate chips.

"I'm sure the roads are plowed now," Krista said, as she stood and carried her dirty dishes to the sink. "You'll have a smooth ride home."

"I'm not leaving yet," Adam said. He took his dishes to the sink, too, planning to help her wash them up later. "I'll help you shovel first."

"There's no need," she protested. "It's not a big deal."

"No arguments, Krista." He tucked in his white shirt and figured the tuxedo pants would have to be good enough to stand a little snow. The shoes would be useless, but he didn't care. With two of them working, the job shouldn't take nearly as long. "I'm not leaving until we've finished shoveling the sidewalk."

She rolled her eyes in annoyance and stomped to the closet. She rummaged around in there and came up with a spare pair of gloves and a hat. "I don't have any boots that will fit you," she said, eyeing his feet. "Although maybe Mr Baumgartner's boots would work."

"I'll be fine." He wasn't desperate enough to take the old man's boots. He pulled on his coat and the borrowed hat and gloves. Krista looked cute, her blonde-streaked curls peeking out of her cap, framing her face, and it took every ounce of his self-control not to haul her into his arms for a kiss.

Krista led him around to the back of the apartment building, where a tiny shed with yard tools was located. She opened the shed and pulled out two snow shovels, handing one to him.

"I'm surprised Mr Baumgartner doesn't have a snow blower," he said, as they buckled down to work. "Seems like even a guy his age should be able to handle a small snow blower."

"I think he did once, but it broke. And when I volunteered to take over, for a deduction on my rent, he agreed." Krista's cheeks were red and she was smiling as she threw a load of heavy wet snow off to the side. "I really don't mind. It's a great excuse to get outside."

He had to agree—there wasn't all that much to do

and the cold, crisp air was refreshing. They worked side by side in companionable silence, finishing most of the sidewalks out back, then going around to the front. When they'd finished, he took her shovel along with his and carried them both back toward the shed.

Before he could put them away, a snowball connected with the back of his head, sliding with icy coldness down his neck.

"What the heck?" He spun around, dropping the shovels, expecting to see a couple of kids. Krista giggled uncontrollably, radiating guilt. Bending down, he grabbed a handful of snow and packed it into a round ball. "You're in trouble now," he threatened, taking a step closer. "If you ask my brothers, they'll tell you I always win when it comes to snowball fights."

"Oh, yeah?" She swung her arm and another snowball hit him square in the chest. "Not this time," she shouted, before turning to run.

He took aim and let loose, his snowball hitting its mark in the center of her back. She let out a squeal and then scooped up more snow, spinning around to retaliate. Her next throw went wide. With a competitive grin he threw another one, hitting her in the side of her head. He felt a momentary pang of guilt when she yelled, "Ouch."

Thankfully she was laughing and gathering more snow, so he relaxed. A snowball came barreling at his head and he ducked just in time to avoid the full blast hitting him in the face.

That had been too close. With a narrowed gaze he gathered up a huge snowball and took off after her. His shoes slipped and slid in the snow, but he managed to catch up to her regardless. Ignoring the cold, he tackled her, taking her down with him into a snow bank.

"Adam!" Her laughter was infectious. He'd planned to wash her face with a fistful of snow but, gazing down at her, snowflakes covering her eyelashes, her cheeks red and her lips parted invitingly, he forgot his original intent. In a heartbeat the playful atmosphere changed to something heated, and he lowered his head to kiss her.

So good. She tasted so good, he couldn't help delving deep, sweeping his tongue into the warmth of her mouth, demanding more. All the need he'd kept under wraps during the night came tumbling out with a rush. The thick layers of winter clothing between them annoyed the hell out of him—he wanted to feel every inch of Krista's body against his.

Her arms wrapped around his neck, pulling him close as she returned his kiss with such enthusiasm he was surprised the snow wasn't evaporating into steam around them.

"Krista," he murmured against her lips. "You're going to get cold. We can't do this here. Come inside with me."

"Yes." She gazed at him with such desire his legs went weak. Or maybe it was just that his tuxedo trousers were soaking wet from lying with her in the snow. Pulling himself together, he levered himself off her and held out a hand to help her up. He quickly returned the snow shovels to the shed and then took her hand, walking back into the apartment building with her.

Inside her apartment he peeled off his coat, hat and gloves, leaving them in a damp pile next to the door. Krista did the same and as soon as she dropped her coat, he pulled her close for another kiss.

"Your clothes are soaked," she whispered.

"I know." Realizing his wet clothes were making her cold, he lifted his head and held her gaze with his as he first took off his shirt and then unfastened his tuxedo trousers, letting them drop to the floor. His black silk boxers were practically invisible when it came to hiding the evidence of his desire.

Krista lifted off her sweater and he sucked in a harsh breath at how beautiful she looked in a sheer pink bra. He didn't bother waiting for her to start on her jeans but swept her into his arms, pressing her beautifully round breasts against his chest.

"I want you so much," he murmured against her mouth. He pulled back enough to look deeply into her eyes. "Are you sure about this? I promised myself I wouldn't take advantage of you."

"I'm sure. I've been wishing for this since last night." Impossibly, his body tightened further at her bold admission. She didn't try to hide the flare of desire in her brown eyes. He debated taking her to the sofa, which was closer, but knew she'd probably be more comfortable in her bed. Before he could move to lift her in his arms, though, his cellphone rang.

He ignored it, but Krista was already pulling back, reaching for the phone he'd left on the counter. "You'd better answer. What if it's about Joy?"

When he took the phone, he realized there were several missed calls from his brother. Keeping his arm around Krista's waist, not wanting to let her go even for a moment, he pushed the speed-dial button to connect to his brother. "Alec? What's up?"

"Adam, we found her."

"Found who?" He couldn't imagine what his brother was talking about.

"The scarf woman. Her name is Nancy Williamson and, according to the birth records down at the Milwaukee courthouse, she gave birth to a baby girl named Joy Williamson eight weeks ago." Alec's voice held a note of excitement. "You were right, Adam. Your mystery woman is Joy's mother."

CHAPTER ELEVEN

KRISTA held her breath as she listened to Alec's voice on the other end of the line.

They'd found Joy's mother?

A mixture of emotions battered her chest. Relief, gladness, wariness, apprehension. Of course, the best thing for Joy would be to be reunited with her mother. But what if her mother had other problems they weren't aware of? What if her mother was ill? Feeling cold about all the possibilities, she pulled away from Adam as he continued his conversation with his brother. On one hand, she was thrilled to discover Joy wasn't all alone in the world.

But she couldn't ignore the tendrils of dread curling in her stomach. She knew firsthand that all homes were not created equal. That the people who were supposed to love and care for children often didn't.

That blood was not always thicker than water.

"I'm sick of taking care of these brats. It's someone else's turn to suffer. I don't care what you say, I'm dropping them off. Today!"

She slammed a door on the painful memory. One of many, although her Aunt Rhonda had been by far the worst, the way she'd screamed at them on a regular basis. She shook her head, trying to dislodge the buzzing in her ears. Vaguely, she realized Adam had ended his call with his brother.

"You found Joy's mother?" She picked up her discarded sweater and held it in front of her scantily clad chest like a shield.

"We think so, but we need to talk to her first." Adam's brow furrowed and he took a step toward her. "Krista, what's wrong?"

"Nothing." She hated the defensive note in her tone. "I'm glad you found Joy's mother. Are you going to see her now?"

"That was the plan." He eyed her warily, as if he'd forgotten he wore only his boxers. "I'm meeting with Alec in an hour. Why?"

"Good." She turned her back to slip on her sweater and ran her fingers through her tousled curls. Crossing her arms over her chest, she faced him, her chin set at a stubborn angle. "I'm coming with you."

There was a long moment of silence before Adam reached for his clothes. He grimaced as he pulled on his wet tuxedo trousers and she squashed a twinge of sympathy.

"Don't you trust me, Krista? I'm not going to hand Joy over unless I'm convinced it's in her best interests." He drew on his white shirt but didn't bother with the buttons.

Trust him? The notion brought her up short. She did trust Adam, they'd very nearly made love just a few moments ago. But she still needed to meet Joy's mother for herself. She wouldn't be able to rest until she knew for sure Joy's mother really loved and cared about Joy. "I know. I'd like to come. Please."

"Of course," he said, taking a step towards the door. "Come on, then. I just need to run home and change first."

"All right." She reached for her coat, and followed him out the door.

Outside, they trudged to his car, parked in the small lot behind the building. As she settled in the passenger seat, her stomach fluttered nervously in anticipation of meeting Joy's mother.

She wished there was time to go and see Joy one last time. To hold the baby close, nuzzling her downy, soft head. To watch her smile as she waved her arms over her head, batting the mobile strung over her crib.

To kiss her satiny-soft cheek, breathing in her soft baby scent.

Tears threatened and she blinked them back with an effort. This wasn't about her wishes but about what was best for Joy. Adam was right. Surely Joy's mother had missed the baby, too. Everything was going to be just fine. She trusted Adam to do what was right.

Glancing over at Adam's strong profile, she couldn't help remembering how his eyes had darkened with passion when he'd kissed her. How his voice had lowered, thick with desire.

She was happy they'd found Joy's mother. But she wished Alec had waited a little longer before calling.

Adam was keenly aware of Krista sitting beside him as he drove to Alec's house. He'd already gone home to change, leaving Krista to gaze around his condo in awe.

It took him a moment to realize she'd never been to his place. He hadn't consciously kept her out of his home, but the result was still the same.

He glanced at her, wishing they could go back to the time before Alec's phone call. He couldn't remember ever having so much fun in the snow. Couldn't remember ever wanting a woman as much as he'd wanted her.

Pulling up in front of Alec's house, he waited for his brother. Alec's brows shot up in surprise when he saw Krista sitting there, but he climbed into the back seat without complaint.

"Hi, Krista," Alec greeted her.

"Hi." Adam thought her smile was strained as he merged with traffic.

"Do you think we should go to Nancy Williamson's house?" he asked Alec, glancing at his brother through the rear-view mirror.

"Yeah, it's our best bet," Alec agreed.

Krista frowned. "You know where she lives?"

"I know the last known address listed for Nancy Williamson," he admitted, deciding not to explain about the night he'd followed the poor woman home on the bus. "But we don't know if she's still living there or not."

He found the address Alec had given him, a tiny house located a few blocks from the bus stop. He parked alongside the curb and then climbed out, taking in their surroundings.

"A 'for sale' sign?" Krista asked in a dismayed tone.

He had to admit, it didn't look good. The "for sale" sign hung on a post at a crooked angle and the tiny bungalow was in desperate need of a new coat of paint, as well as a new roof.

Nancy Williamson had clearly fallen on desperate times.

Exchanging a concerned glance with Alec and Krista, he strode up to the door and knocked.

No answer. With a frown, he rang the doorbell, listening as it pealed throughout the house. Still no one came to the door.

"Where is she?" Krista asked in a plaintive tone.

"I don't know." Adam frowned and glanced around at the neighboring houses. "Alec, what do you think?"

His brother shrugged. "The cop who talked to her boss at the discount store said she left for home right after work."

"Are you sure?" Adam persisted. Alec had told him that Nancy had a job at the discount store located near the bus stop. And within walking distance from his clinic. "Maybe she's working later than he thought?"

Alec sighed. "I'm sure."

"Should we wait?" Krista asked, rubbing her gloved hands together to generate warmth. "It's freezing out here."

"No, we won't wait," Adam said. "But we can at least leave a note. Maybe she's scared, worried that we're going to arrest her or something." Adam glanced around. "Do either of you have a paper and pencil?"

"I do." Alec pulled out his small notebook.

Adam wrote a note, trying to keep it short, explaining how he wanted to help, that Joy was doing fine and was being cared for at Children's Memorial Hospital. He scrawled his name on the bottom and shoved the note into the crack in the door.

He stared at it for a long moment. What if she really didn't live here any more and didn't get his message?

"I hope she sees it," Krista said in a worried tone, reading his thoughts.

"Me, too," Adam agreed.

Alec clapped a hand on Adam's shoulder. "Hey, relax. It's not the end of the world just because we couldn't talk to her today. We know her name. We'll find her. If not tomorrow, then on Monday."

"Monday?" Krista echoed in dismay. "That long?"

"We'll find her," Alec repeated.

Adam jammed his fists in his coat pockets, knowing his brother was right. There was no rush, other than his own anxiety in needing to meet the woman who'd abandoned her baby in his clinic. To prove that he'd done the right thing in tracking her down, intent on reuniting mother and daughter.

Krista was quiet as they trooped back to the car. He wished he could say something to make her feel better about all this. Given the way she'd grown up, he understood her reservations about Joy's mother.

Krista was a kind-hearted soul, a woman who cared for others deeply. He'd caught a glimpse of her compassion when she'd cared for her Aunt Bea. He knew she'd grown too attached to Joy—she hadn't even been able to start an IV on the baby.

Everything he knew about Krista convinced him she longed for a family. Hadn't she admitted as much when explaining how she'd applied to be a temporary receiving home? Joy wasn't the only baby Krista had fallen for—there'd been at least one other, too. And even if Joy was reunited with her mother, there was always the possibility of another abandoned baby or orphaned child needing help.

Krista would always make room in her heart for children. Especially children in need.

She was the kind of woman who deserved the whole package—a ring, marriage, and a family.

The knowledge sat heavily in his gut.

He'd almost had a family once, and still hadn't quite recovered from the loss.

He wasn't at all sure he'd ever be ready to try again.

The next day, Krista was scheduled to work second shift, starting at three, but left her apartment complex early so that she could spend some time with Joy.

She walked into Joy's room, half expecting to find Joy's mother had arrived, but Joy was alone in her crib. Staring down at the happy baby, she thought about how desolate the house had seemed yesterday, with the crooked "for sale" sign out front.

Where was Joy's mother? Hopefully not living in the street. She couldn't bear to think of the poor woman having no home.

When Joy saw her, she waved her arms excitedly. Krista tried not to put too much stock in thinking Joy could actually recognize her, but still grinned and leaned over to pick up the baby. "Hi, there," she crooned, pressing a kiss to Joy's temple. "Are you feeling lonely? I have almost a full hour to spend with you before the start of my shift."

Krista settled herself into the rocker with Joy on her lap. She faced the baby as she spoke, the way the books on deafness had told her to. She wished there was more she could do to help Joy begin dealing with her deafness. Did Joy's mother realize the baby was deaf? Despite Adam's assurances otherwise, she wasn't so sure.

Joy was clearly feeling better. The baby made faces, making Krista laugh when a fountain of bubbles gathered around her mouth. She was eating better, too. Krista was pleased to see Joy had actually gained a couple of pounds since she'd first been admitted.

Had it only been two and a half weeks since the night she and Adam had worked together to care for Joy? It hardly seemed possible. Thoughts of Adam caused her smile to fade.

She'd bared her soul about her past but she still didn't know very much about him. It was easy to admire his work as a pediatrician, yet at the same time it bothered her, the way he held himself aloof. Was he that way just with her, or with everyone? All she knew for sure was that even when it came to Joy, he managed to keep a safe, comfortable distance, never getting too close. He'd even gone so far as to warn her about getting too attached.

Adam came from a loud, noisy family, yet she thought it was odd how he hadn't once mentioned ever having children of his own.

He'd asked if she trusted him, and she did. But apparently he didn't reciprocate by trusting her. At least, not enough to share his hopes, his dreams, or his emotions.

The knowledge rubbed like salt in a wound.

He didn't care for her the way she cared about him.

The hour was late, a few minutes past three, so she quickly stood and carried Joy back to her crib. "I'll stop back to see you soon, sweetheart," she promised. "Be good, now."

She turned away, certain that this was probably the

last time she'd see Joy. Even if for some monumental reason Joy's mother didn't return, Adam was still likely to discharge the baby on Monday. Clearly, Joy no longer needed medical care.

"There you are!" Amy called, when she walked into the nurses' station. "We've been worried about you."

"I'm here." She forced a smile. "Have you already assigned me some patients?" She fully expected they had. It was her fault she was late, having dawdled in Joy's room.

"Yes, you have the new admission being sent up from the ED." Amy handed her a slip of paper. "Meagan took report for you. The four-month-old baby was treated with some antibiotics for an ear infection and had some sort of allergic response." Amy turned back toward the assignment board. "In addition to that, we gave you the Simmons baby, he's only four weeks old and has a low-grade fever. And little Olivia is having tests for early kidney failure."

All of her patients were young but, sometimes the other nurses fought over who would get to take care of the toddlers. However, she didn't mind the infants. "Sounds good. When is the new admission due to arrive?"

There was a commotion in the hallway as a crib was rolled onto the unit. "I think that's her now."

"Cynthia Downer has a rash covering most of her body, after receiving two doses of penicillin," the ED physician informed her. There was a tiny woman, obviously Cynthia's mother, walking alongside the crib. "I think the main reason Dr Monroe wanted her admitted was to watch for signs of respiratory failure."

The baby was Adam's patient? It shouldn't have

been a big surprise, she needed to learn how to maintain a professional relationship with him unless she planned to quit her job, which she didn't.

She loved taking care of kids.

"Sounds good." She flashed a smile at Cynthia's mother. "Hello, my name is Krista, and I'll be Cynthia's nurse. Let's get her settled into her room, shall we?" Krista led the way to the room next to Joy's. Once the crib was placed up against the wall, she dropped the side and began to examine the baby. The ED physician, Dr Luis Garcia, hadn't been kidding about the rash. She'd never seen such a bright redness covering the entire torso before.

Krista pulled out her stethoscope and listened to Cynthia's lungs. She frowned, and glanced up at Luis. "I hear wheezes in both bases."

"Really?" Luis took out his stethoscope and listened, too. His expression turned serious. "Those wheezes weren't there before. You'd better page Adam."

"Is he on call?" she asked, reaching for the phone.

"Yes. Actually, this patient belongs to one of his partners." Luis glanced down at the baby.

"Is she going to be all right?" Cynthia's mother asked in alarm.

"We're doing everything we can," Krista assured her. She asked the operator to page Adam, and then glanced at Luis. "Can you get me a syringe of epinephrine before you leave? Just in case?"

"Sure." He disappeared from the room.

Krista turned back to her tiny patient and a very worried mother. "We really need to keep an eye on Cynthia's breathing. If anything changes at all, we're going to need to treat her for anaphylactic shock."

Cynthia's mother bit her lip and nodded. Krista connected a pulse-ox machine to the baby's forehead, getting an initial reading of 92 per cent. A little on the low side, and she used her stethoscope to listen again.

The baby's lungs sounded worse. Even as she watched, the baby's pulse ox dropped lower and lower. The skin around Cynthia's lips took on a bluish tinge.

It was enough to scare her. "I'm calling a code," she told Cynthia's mother. She turned toward the phone just as Adam walked in.

"Thank heavens you're here. She's about to go into respiratory arrest."

"Get the crash cart, its right outside in the hall," he ordered.

She ran out to grab the crash cart. Luis returned to the room at the moment with a syringe of epinephrine. After twisting off the plastic lock, she opened the bottom drawer where the emergency airway equipment was located.

"Hand me the laryngoscope," Adam told her.

She locked the laryngoscope blade on the handle and gave it to him. "Do you want me to call the rest of the code team?"

"Yes. In case I have trouble intubating her."

"I'll do it." Luis picked up the phone.

More nurses entered the room and Krista was glad one of them went over to comfort Cynthia's mother.

"Give her one milligram per kilogram of epinephrine intramuscularly," Adam said.

Krista didn't hesitate but grabbed the fleshy part of the baby's thigh and gave the injection.

Adam managed to get the tiny breathing tube placed before the rest of the code team arrived. In moments the room was flooded with people. The pediatric anesthesiologist peered at the breathing tube and the subsequently improved pulse-ox readings and nodded.

"Good job," he said to Adam, before turning to leave.

Krista felt her own heart rate slowly return to normal. This was way too much excitement for the start of her day. More people filtered out of the room, realizing the worst of the emergency had passed. Krista turned to Adam. "Do you want me to arrange for Cynthia's transfer to PICU?"

"Yeah." He nodded, sending her a look of gratitude. "Thanks."

"No problem." She made yet another phone call, realizing as she did so how she and Adam still made a great team. The moment was bitter-sweet. She spoke to the PICU nurse, informing her of the transfer, watching as Adam explained everything that had just happened to Cynthia's mother. When the woman began to cry, he put his arm around her and let her cry on his shoulder.

Krista hung up the phone, her chest tight. Cynthia would be fine, thanks to Adam. He was a great pediatrician with so much to give.

Too bad he only dished out servings of emotional care to his patients.

He could have used some for his personal life as well.

CHAPTER TWELVE

KRISTA didn't see Adam again for several hours, although that didn't stop her from watching for him. Concentrating on her small patients was more than enough to keep her busy.

She obtained Olivia's urine specimen and sent it to the lab. The baby with suspected kidney failure certainly seemed fine, but the way her creatinine was creeping upward was concerning enough to keep her in the hospital until all the tests were complete.

Little Frankie Simmons worried her. He was the one-month-old baby who'd been admitted with a low-grade fever. When she'd first taken his temperature, it had been 38. Only now his temperature had bumped up to 38.8.

Holding the baby in her arms, she called Dr Strong, Frankie's pediatrician, to inform him of the spike in Frankie's fever. He ordered a lumbar-puncture procedure to rule out aseptic meningitis. "Ask the ED resident to do it and then call me back with the results."

"I will." She glanced down at Frankie, thinking how small he looked. His mother had run home for a few hours to check on her three-year-old twins, and she debated calling Mrs Simmons to let her know. Actually, as the procedure would likely be over before she could return to the hospital, it was probably better this way. LPs were not easy procedures for parents to watch.

Adam walked into the nurses' station while she was waiting for Luis Garcia to return her page. She glanced at the clock, surprised to see him as it was well past seven p.m. "You're still here?"

"Yeah." He flashed a tired smile. "Lots of sick kids have been admitted over the past few days. It took me a while to make rounds on them all."

"I see." Even exhausted, he exuded an attractiveness that made her glance away and swallow hard. Why was she so in tune with his presence? To his every mood? When the phone rang, she pounced on it. "Six South, Krista speaking."

"This is Luis Garcia. Did someone page me?"

"I did. Thanks for calling me back. I have a four-week-old infant by the name of Frankie Simmons who needs a lumbar puncture procedure. Can you come up to do it?"

"We're pretty swamped down here at the moment, and we're short a resident because someone called in sick. I'll do my best to get up there, but it may take me a few hours."

"A few hours?" she echoed in dismay. "For a lumbar puncture?"

"I'm sorry." Luis did actually sound apologetic. "All I can do is promise to be up as soon as I can."

"I understand." She blew out her breath in a sigh. "Thanks." She hung up the phone.

"Something wrong?" Adam asked.

"No." She smoothed a hand down Frankie's back.

The baby was a virtual heating pad. Thinking of his fever only made her more frustrated. "This little guy needs an LP, but the ED is swamped. Dr Garcia promised to get up here as soon as he can."

"I'll do it."

She blinked at his offer. "You will?"

"Why not? I'm here and have the time."

She remembered the night Joy had been admitted, how Adam had done her LP then, too. As an attending physician, he was certainly capable of doing the lumbar puncture, but Frankie wasn't his patient. She hesitated. Was there some rule about this? "As Frankie's not your patient, I should probably wait until Luis can get here."

"Who's the pediatrician of record?" Adam asked.

"Dr Ronald Strong." She handed him Frankie's chart.

"I know Ron pretty well. I'll call him. I'm sure he won't mind."

She didn't know what to say as Adam called his acquaintance and explained the situation. She couldn't understand why he was being so nice. Surely he had other things to do than to worry about her patients. Especially considering he'd already spent a good portion of his Sunday here at the hospital. She would have thought he'd be dying to get home by now.

When he hung up the phone a few minutes later, he wrote a note on the chart. "Ron is happy to have me perform the procedure. I've made a notation in the chart to cover us in case anyone asks."

"Adam, why are you doing this?" She glanced around, making sure no one could overhear them behind the nurses' station. "Frankie's LP isn't your problem."

"Because I don't like to see you upset." Adam's smile was crooked and the intensity of his gaze made her realize he was doing this for her. And, of course, for Frankie. "It's not a big deal. Shall we get started?"

"Yes." She wasn't going to argue because she honestly didn't want Frankie to have to wait for his procedure. She led the way down the hall to Frankie's room and laid the baby down in his crib so she could gather the necessary supplies together. Adam helped, arranging his LP tray the way he liked it. As before, they worked very well as a team. When she'd gotten everything they needed, she fetched Frankie and strapped him securely to the procedure table.

"What's his latest temp?" Adam asked as he began to unwrap the sterile LP tray.

"Almost 39." She undressed the little guy who began to cry, not liking his heated body exposed to the air. "Shh, now, it's OK. I'm here for you."

Adam glanced at her but didn't say anything. He donned a pair of sterile gloves from the LP kit and used the antimicrobial solution to wash Frankie's back. She tightened her grip on the baby when he lifted the long, thin spinal needle.

"Ready?" Adam met her gaze.

She nodded and held her breath, wondering how on earth Adam could find the column of cerebral spinal fluid in such a small baby. But he did, just as he had with Joy, on the first stick.

"I'm ready for the first tube."

She handed him the tubes in order and he put a few drops of spinal fluid into each one. When he'd finished, she drew a deep breath of relief. "Thanks, Adam."

"You're welcome." His deep voice reminded her of the fun they'd had, playing in the snow. He'd laughed when she hit him with that snowball and he'd surprised her when he'd sought revenge by tackling her.

Mostly she remembered the heated kisses that had practically melted the snow around them.

She forced the images away. This wasn't the time to think about why she liked him so much. "Have you talked to Joy's mother?"

He cast her a quick glance, and then shook his head. "No, not yet. I stopped by this morning, but she wasn't home."

"She wasn't?" She frowned, not liking the implication. "Adam, what if something has happened to her?"

"Try not to think the worst. We'll find her."

She'd try, but it wouldn't be easy. After washing the antibiotic solution off Frankie's back, she dressed him in his navy blue sleeper. When she'd finished, she set him in the crib, so she could get the tubes of fluid sent to the lab.

"Do you need anything else?" Adam asked as she labeled each of the tubes with Frankie's name and medical record number.

"No, but thanks. You've been a huge help." She smiled and gestured to Frankie. "Now at least I can start his antibiotics, just in case he does have bacterial meningitis."

Adam glanced around. "I guess I'd better go. Are you working tomorrow?"

"All week." She kept her tone cheerful.

"I'll see you tomorrow, then." He turned to leave.

She watched him go, wishing she could call him back.

Because she'd never felt so lonely in her entire life. Not when Danielle had told her she was heading off to a modeling job in London. Not when Aunt Bea had passed away quietly in her sleep.

She missed the closeness she shared with Adam but she wouldn't be satisfied with just a little part of him, the part he chose to share.

She wanted everything. Especially his love.

She managed to keep from dwelling on Adam too much as the end of her shift loomed near. She was finishing with Frankie's bath when Luis strode into the room.

"I'm sorry it took me so long," he said. "It was a really rough night. There were back-to-back car accidents involving small kids." His dark eyes held pain. "We lost one of them, a five-year-old boy."

"I'm so sorry." Put in perspective, those trauma victims had needed Luis's help far more than Frankie had. The lines of fatigue etched in his face convinced her he hadn't simply been putting her off.

He forced a smile. "Not your fault."

"It is, because I made you rush up here for nothing." She gave him an apologetic glance. "I don't need your help after all. Luckily Dr Monroe was here and he did Frankie's LP for me."

"I'm glad." Luis gazed down at the baby. "I really felt awful about taking so long. It seemed like the stream of patients just wouldn't end. And those last two trauma patients were bad. The little girl is still in surgery, we're still not sure she'll make it."

"Hey, it's OK." She touched his arm, trying to make him feel better. As much as she loved her job, she couldn't imagine working down in the ED with trauma patients. Especially small children. "You can go back down and get caught up."

"Yeah." Luis shook off his somber mood and glanced at his watch. "Actually, I only have another hour of my shift left to go. How about you?"

Puzzled, she nodded. "I'm off at eleven-thirty, too."

"Would you like to stop for a drink after work?" His invitation caught her off guard. Was he looking for someone to talk to after his rough shift in the ED? If so, she couldn't blame him. "There's a nice little pub down the street and they serve a great hot chocolate laced with peppermint schnapps."

Luis Garcia was a very attractive man, his dark hair and bright smile enough to charm any woman. As much as she wished she could go with him, she knew it wouldn't be fair.

Not when her heart still ached for Adam.

"I'm sorry, but I can't tonight," she murmured in regret.

He didn't take offense. "I understand. Maybe another time?"

"Sure." If someday she managed to get over Adam, she wouldn't mind seeing Luis away from the hospital.

At the door of Frankie's room he turned to glance back at her. "Krista? Good catch on those wheezes earlier. You really helped save that little girl's life."

"Thanks." She was surprised by his compliment. Before she could say anything more, he flashed that sinful smile again and left.

Luis was a great guy. A few months ago she would have been thrilled to go with him for a drink after work.

A few months ago she hadn't been nearly as self-confident, in her nursing abilities or on a personal level.

But not any more. For the first time she realized she didn't feel as if she were still sitting in Danielle's shadow. She was a competent pediatric nurse and a desirable woman.

Too bad her heart was set on the one man who didn't want her in the same way she wanted him.

Adam couldn't get Krista out of his mind. After he'd gone home the previous night, he'd thought about her until he'd fallen asleep, and she was the first thing that popped into his mind when he woke up the next morning.

He needed to talk to her. Soon. Today. He needed to tell her about the accident and about losing his son. She deserved the truth.

And he needed her absolution.

When he walked into the clinic he heard the Christmas song "Winter Wonderland" and immediately thought of Krista. He could still see her so clearly in his mind, holding Joy and humming along as the carolers sang.

Great. At this rate he'd never get her out of his head.

Luckily, the clinic schedule was surprisingly light, maybe because tomorrow was Christmas Eve, so most people were only coming in if their child was really sick. As he took a quick break for lunch, his mother called, demanding to know if he'd invited Krista to the annual Monroe holiday gathering on Christmas Day.

"She can't come, she's working."

"She's working?" His mother's disappointment radiated over the line. "Can't she get it off?"

"You know someone has to work the holiday, Mom," he said in a gentle tone. He'd done his share of holidays, as had Abby and Alaina. "I'm sure all the nurses would love to have the day off. I'll ask her again, just in case she's really not needed."

"All right." His mother sighed. "See you on Wednesday, Adam."

"I'll be there," he promised, before hanging up the phone.

He stared at it for a moment. His mother wasn't the only one disappointed to know Krista had to work the holiday.

He wanted to share Christmas with her, too.

Krista had a way of making him forget the sadness of the holiday. Hadn't she instigated that snowball fight? It had been years since he'd had fun playing in the snow.

His body tightened with memories of what had nearly happened after the snowball fight. Shaking off the remnants of desire, he stood and prepared to see his next patient. At the end of his clinic he'd head over to the hospital to make rounds.

So far there hadn't been any word on Joy's mother. Alec had promised to go over there some time today. He was beginning to suspect Nancy wasn't living in the tiny bungalow any more. But where was she? As far as Alec could figure out, she didn't have family, but maybe she'd moved in with a friend. Regardless of where she was living, he'd have to discharge Joy soon. He was only holding off because he still hoped Nancy would show.

His next patient was a tall, gangly, adolescent girl who was complaining of a sore throat. Her throat was very red and inflamed, but he didn't know for sure if the cause was a strep infection or possibly mononucleosis.

"We'll have to test Ericka for both strep and mono," he told her mother. "If it's strep, we can give her antibiotics and she'll feel better in a few days. If it's mono, there isn't much we can do other than treat her symptoms."

"Oh, dear." Ericka's mother looked concerned. "If she has mono, do we need to cancel our Christmas plans?"

"Let's wait and see what she has first," Adam hedged. Mono was pretty infectious, but he didn't want to borrow trouble. While he waited for the lab work to be run, he saw another patient and ordered more antibiotics. Some days it seemed as if he was running a special on them. After the lab tests had been run, he went back into the room.

"I'm afraid Ericka does have mono," he told them. "I hate to ruin your holiday, but she really shouldn't have contact with other kids right now. At least, not for the next week or so."

"Oh, Ericka." Her mother gave her a quick hug.

Ericka's expression was glum. "That's OK, Mom. You can go to Grandma and Grandpa's house without me. Everyone will be there. I don't want to wreck your Christmas."

"Don't be silly. We love you. We're not going without you," her mother chided. "We'll get together another time, maybe for New Year, when you're feeling better."

"Good idea." Adam smiled.

He thought about what Ericka had said, about not wanting to wreck Christmas. Hadn't he been doing the same thing, avoiding telling Krista the upsetting details about the accident, and especially his role in it, because he didn't want to wreck her faith in him?

He had to believe she'd be there for him, no matter what.

Adam finished with his last patient just after three-thirty. Perfect timing, as he wanted to check on Joy and hopefully run into Krista at the same time. At least, he was assuming she was working the evening shift again today.

Maybe they could grab a quick break together and talk. Now that he'd made up his mind to tell her, he was impatient to see her.

It was brutally cold outside, and the only bright spot in the sub-zero temperatures was that it was too cold to snow. He pulled up the collar of his coat as he walked from the parking lot to the hospital.

On the sixth floor, he went down to the south wing and headed straight to Joy's room. He stopped inside the doorway when his gaze caught Krista rocking Joy to sleep.

His heart squeezed in his chest. She looked so beautiful. A perfect mother for his children.

Whoa, wait a minute. His children? Since losing his son, he hadn't thought about having more children.

The tension around his heart eased. Somehow it was easier to imagine a future with Krista at his side.

He cleared his throat and knocked on the door. "Hi, Krista."

"Hi." She stopped rocking, looking flustered. "Are you here alone?" She glanced past him, as if expecting someone to be standing beside him. Like Joy's mother? "Did you need to examine Joy?"

"Yes." He wasn't sure he could put off discharging the baby much longer. He'd have to talk to Shirley to see what his options were. Maybe the state wouldn't mind if he waited until the day after Christmas. "How are you?"

"Me?" She carried Joy over to the crib. "I'm fine."

Before he could ask her anything more, his cell-phone rang. He recognized Alec's number. Finally. He flipped open the phone. "Alec? Have you found her yet?"

"Adam, this is Abby. I'm using Alec's phone." His sister sounded upset, her nose stuffed up as if she'd been crying. "We're here at Trinity Medical Center with Jillian. She's bleeding, Adam." Abby's voice hitched. "It's possible she's losing the baby."

CHAPTER THIRTEEN

KRISTA knew something was wrong when Adam's face paled, his expression turning as hard as granite.

He didn't so much as glance at her. "I'll be right there," he said, seconds before he hung up the phone, already heading towards the door.

"Adam, wait." She caught the sleeve of his leather jacket. "What is it? What's wrong?"

"Jillian might be losing the baby." His terse voice cut deep. "I have to go."

"Wait for me. I'll come with you." Thank heavens she had switched shifts to cover a sick call and had worked the day shift. She grabbed her purse, thinking they could stop at the staff locker room on the way out to fetch her coat. "I'll only be a minute."

"No." Adam's abrupt tone stopped her, especially when he pulled out of her grasp. "There's no need. It's better if I go alone."

Better to go alone? For whom? Stunned, she stared at him as he walked out of Joy's room without looking back.

His abrupt dismissal hurt. More than she'd ever thought possible. Once again he'd emotionally withdrawn from her, shutting her out of his life at a time of crisis.

Did she need more proof that he wasn't interested in a long-term relationship? Seemed he'd made his intentions pretty clear.

Sick at the realization, she sank into the rocking chair.

Adam didn't need her. He certainly didn't love her.

Not the way she loved and needed him.

Adam strode down the hall of Trinity Medical Center to the waiting area located on the seventh floor where the labor and delivery unit was located.

He wasn't surprised to see most of his family already gathered there. His parents were seated beside each other, his father's strong arm hooked around his mother's shoulders. Abby and Nick were there, along with Alaina and her husband Scott. Shelby sat next to Bethany and Ben, Alaina and Scott's kids.

The mood in the room was understandably somber. His mother's eyes looked suspiciously bright, as if she might have been crying. Even the kids were unnaturally quiet. Standing at the back of the room, his back against the wall, he was glad he hadn't taken Krista up on her offer to skip work to come with him. The situation here with his family was already awkward enough.

He knew, more than anyone, just how helpless Alec was feeling now.

"Have we heard anything yet?" he asked, breaking the silence.

"No." Abby lifted her head from her husband's chest, lines of concern bracketing her mouth. "Alec said he'd let us know when he had news."

"A little spotting doesn't always mean the pregnancy is in trouble," his mother said in a soft tone. "I had spotting with my second pregnancy, too, and Alaina is proof that everything worked out in the long run."

"I didn't realize that," Alaina said. Adam figured she was trying to remain positive for Shelby's sake. "I'll be more than happy to find out we've all been sitting here worrying over nothing."

He would, too, Adam thought, but he didn't believe it. The nauseous feeling in his stomach reminded him too much of the past. Glancing at Abby and Nick, he could see his younger sister didn't believe it either.

Time seemed to stand still. He could swear every glance at the clock showed it was barely two minutes since the last time he'd checked.

After what seemed like for ever, Alec walked in, his shoulders slumped and his expression grim. He went straight over to Shelby and pulled her into his arms for a hug.

"I'm sorry, Jillian lost the baby," he said in a choked voice.

"No!" Shelby cried, burying her face against Alec's chest, her little shoulders shaking with sobs.

"Shh, it's alright," Alec soothed, maintaining a brave front, although Adam could tell his brother was close to losing it as well. "Hey, there's a reason this happened. The baby wasn't strong enough to survive. Jillian is fine. The doctor said we can try again in a few months." He smoothed a hand down Shelby's hair. "Don't cry, Shelby. Please, don't cry."

Adam glanced away, unable to bear his brother's pain. The situation with Jillian was very different from what he'd experienced. She'd only been eleven weeks pregnant, not twenty-four, as Danielle had been.

And Jillian hadn't lost her baby as a result of his carelessness.

"Are they going to discharge Jillian?" Abby asked, her eyes damp with tears.

Alec shook his head. "She's suffered more bleeding than they'd expected, they're even talking about a blood transfusion." He glanced down at Shelby. "Shelby, do you mind staying overnight with Aunt Alaina and Bethany?"

Shelby sniffled and swiped at her eyes. Bravely, she shook her head. "No, I don't mind, Daddy."

Alec sent a questioning glance at Alaina, who hastened to reassure him. "It's no problem having Shelby stay with us, Alec. You know she's always welcome."

"Thanks." Fatigue and sorrow etched grooves in Alec's face.

Adam pushed away from the wall, coming further into the room. "Alec, I know how you feel. Losing a baby, even one that hasn't been born yet, is difficult, but the loss will get easier over time, trust me. I've been in your shoes."

The varying shocked expressions on his family's faces made him realize what he'd just said. For the first time in months he'd mentioned his son.

"You lost a baby, Adam?" Abby asked, pulling away from her husband, Nick. "Who was pregnant?"

"Danielle." He shoved his hands into his pockets, debating whether to tell them the rest. But he couldn't quite bring himself to explain how it had all been his fault. "She was twenty-three weeks pregnant when we were in a car accident last year, right before Christmas.

Our son was stillborn." He glanced at his father. "We didn't have a funeral, but I did name him after you, Dad. Abraham Joseph Monroe."

"Oh, Adam. Why didn't you tell us?" his mother asked.

"Danielle didn't want anyone to know." He glanced at his family, realizing just how much he'd needed their support back then. And now. Seeing his family surrounding Alec and Jillian had driven the point home. "And I couldn't talk about it either." Because the overwhelming guilt had kept the secret festering in his heart. "I'm sorry I didn't tell you sooner."

"No reason to apologize," Alec said, giving Shelby one last hug before rising to his feet. "I need to go back to Jillian, but thanks for telling us. You've actually made me feel lucky that Jillian and I have each other to get through this, which is more than you had."

It was true. Adam knew Alec and Jillian's love would draw them closer together during a time of crisis. They'd support each other, which would only help to ease the pain.

Alec's gaze shifted to someone behind him. He turned in time to see Krista standing in the doorway of the waiting room, her gaze stricken. She'd heard every word.

Guilt seized him as he realized his mistake. He should have told her first.

"Krista," he began, moving to cross over to her, but she spun on her heel and vanished down the hall.

Krista fought tears as she quickened her pace, anxious to put as much distance between herself and Adam as possible.

He'd never told her Danielle had been pregnant.

Hadn't told her about losing his son. Hadn't mentioned his son's name, not once in the time they'd spent together.

What else had he kept from her?

"Krista!" She heard Adam shout from behind her, but she didn't trust herself to turn around. Didn't trust herself not to settle for whatever scraps he'd choose to give her.

She deserved better. Her head knew that much, although her heart felt as if it had been ripped from her chest and shredded into tiny bits.

When she reached the elevator, luck was with her because the doors opened, allowing several people to step out. She slipped past them to go inside, quickly pressing the button to go down. When the elevator didn't move fast enough, she stabbed the button to close the doors even as Adam called her name again.

The doors closed before he reached her. Alone in the elevator, she sagged against the wall, burying her face in her hands, her eyes burning with tears.

She wasn't ready to face him. Not now and not any time soon. Obviously, she couldn't avoid Adam forever, but she needed time. Time to marshal her defenses against him.

Time to convince herself the wisest choice was to get over him, once and for all.

Krista didn't go straight home. Staring at the four walls in her empty apartment didn't hold much appeal. Instead, she headed to the mall, losing herself among the harried Christmas shoppers.

She wandered from store to store, not seeing anything, her stomach knotted to the point of acute pain. She'd thought it had been difficult before, when she'd had a crush on Adam while he'd belonged to Danielle, but this feeling of loss was much, much worse.

Because she loved him. Loved him with her entire heart and soul. And wanted the same in return.

He'd kept so much of his personal feelings hidden away from her. Had Danielle felt the same way? Had Adam refused to share every aspect of his life with her sister? She was still struggling to grasp that her sister had miscarried and never told her. Had Adam pulled away from her then, too? Was his aloofness part of what had broken them up after the miscarriage?

Her head ached with the effort of holding back tears. She really needed to get a grip on her emotions. Feeling this level of acute devastation wasn't healthy.

She stood in front of a bright Christmas display without seeing the flash of lights, the colored ornaments on the tree. Thank heavens she had to work the holiday. Sitting home alone would have been so much worse.

Lost in her misery, she didn't realize how many hours had passed until the mall shops began to close. Glancing at her watch, she saw it was late.

She trudged out to her car, dreading the idea of going home when she really needed someone to talk to. But she didn't have much choice. Flying to London to be with her sister wasn't an option, not when she was committed to work the next few days.

Calling Danielle was a possibility, but London was six hours ahead. If she called Danielle now, it would be close to three or four in the morning there.

No use. She'd have to wait until the morning.

Danielle was a night owl, but not even her sister stayed up on a routine basis until the wee hours of the morning.

Mr Baumgartner was out sprinkling sand on the sidewalks to prevent people from slipping when she got home.

"Goodnight, Mr Baumgartner," she said, slowing her step as she approached.

The older man stared at her. "The Olsons have given their notice, they're moving out of their two-bed apartment on February first. Are you still interested in upgrading your place?"

She paused, realizing there was no need now that Joy's mother had likely been found. Still, she nodded. There was no reason she couldn't still be considered as a temporary receiving home. If not for Joy, then for the next small baby who needed her. She'd have a family, one way or another. "Yes," she said. "I would be interested."

"Fine." Mr Baumgartner shook another handful of sand on the sidewalk. "If for some reason you change your mind, let me know. I won't advertise until after New Year anyway."

"I won't change my mind." She strode past him, using her key to let her into the apartment building.

Instead of going to bed, she sat up for hours, doing the math and figuring out ways she'd financially swing the more expensive two-bedroom apartment the Olsons would be vacating.

She liked the idea of being a temporary receiving home for children in need. Taking control of her life felt good. Or at least dulled the pain of losing Adam.

Losing him wasn't exactly the right term. Obviously, she'd never had him in the first place.

She stared at her notes. One extra overtime shift a pay period would carry her through the next few months, until she had her credit-card bill paid off. After that she'd be in the clear. If she worked hard enough and watched her expenses, she could make it work.

Unlike Adam's feelings toward her, which she couldn't change, no matter how much she wished she could. The way he closed himself off from others, especially from her, was something he needed to change on his own.

If he wanted to.

The next morning Krista dragged herself out of bed with a groan, rubbing her gritty, red-rimmed eyes. She hadn't slept much, but needed to get ready for work. Besides, she wanted to go in early to spend some time with Joy. Plus she needed to bring in the Christmas gifts she'd purchased for the unit.

Her phone rang and she tensed, wondering if the caller was Adam. With trepidation, she picked up the phone. "Hello?"

"Krista?" Danielle's husky voice flowed over the line. "How are you?"

"I'm good, Danielle. I'm glad you called. I was thinking of you last night." She'd actually been thinking about the baby her sister and Adam had lost, but decided this wasn't the time to bring it up. Adam was obviously still upset about the loss, whereas Danielle had moved on.

She couldn't blame her sister for living her life.

"I've been thinking of you, too." Danielle's bubbly tone was infectious. "How do you feel about taking a trip out here to see me?"

It was the first time Danielle had offered to have Krista come and visit. Surprised, she answered, "I'd love to, but I'm not sure I can swing it financially." She'd spent hours last night just trying to figure out a way to make her financial ends meet. "But I do miss you, Danielle. I'd love to see you again."

"I miss you, too." Krista could hear a deep voice in the background. "Marc wants me to say hi. He's the reason I suggested you come out for a visit. He's asked me to marry him and I've accepted."

"Danielle! I'm so happy for you." And she truly was happy for her sister. After everything Danielle had been through, she was glad her sister had found love.

"Thanks, Krista. The wedding isn't going to be until next summer, and I really was hoping you'd stand up as my maid of honor."

"Of course I'll stand up for you." Pleased, she immediately agreed. Summer was months away. If she finagled her finances, she might be able to swing it. If not, she'd put the plane ticket on her credit card and go back to the overtime shifts. "Are you kidding? I wouldn't miss your wedding for anything."

"Great. I'll let you know a date as soon as we've picked one." Danielle laughed. "I had no idea I could be so happy. How are things with you, Krista?"

"Good." She didn't want to dampen Danielle's enthusiasm by bringing up the problems of her love life, yet she needed to at least let Danielle know about Adam. "I like my job at Children's Memorial very much."

"Children's Memorial?" Danielle repeated. "I'm surprised you haven't run into Adam."

"Actually, I have. We've shared a few patients." She held her breath, waiting for Danielle's response.

"How is he?" Danielle asked. "I hope he's found happiness, the way I have."

Krista knew he hadn't but refrained from saying it. "He seems fine. He's a good doctor."

"A good doctor and a great guy," Danielle agreed. "If you see him, tell him I wish him well. He and I weren't good together, he was far too intense for me, but I don't hold any hard feelings against him."

Intense? Odd that Danielle had considered him intense when she'd only seen him as aloof. Had losing his son changed him so much?

"I will," Krista responded, although she wasn't planning to converse with Adam any time soon. "Take care of yourself, Danielle. Give Marc a hug for me and send me some pictures if you have them."

"I do have pictures to send. Check your e-mail later today. Bye, Krista. Merry Christmas."

"Merry Christmas, Danielle." Krista hung up the phone, thinking about what Danielle had said.

Thinking back to the Adam she'd known then to the Adam she knew now, she realized Danielle was right. He'd changed after losing his son. For years she'd thought of him as the perfect man, kind, considerate, always there when she'd needed him.

Yet now she was upset with him because he was human? Because he'd withdrawn, emotionally, after losing his son?

Thoughtful, she glanced at the clock and realized she

needed to hurry to get ready for work. Would she see Adam? If so, she'd better figure out what she was going to say when she saw him.

Her anger and resentment had vanished, she realized as she negotiated her car along the slippery streets on her way to the hospital. She was disappointed and hurt at the way he'd consistently pulled away from her, but she couldn't be angry.

She didn't believe Adam had hurt her on purpose.

In fact, she was convinced he was too busy hurting himself. Possibly out of some misplaced sense of guilt.

At Children's, the staff parking lot was nearly empty. Only the hospital staff who absolutely had to be at work showed up on Christmas Eve.

With a determined stride she hauled the bag of gifts up to the sixth floor. She stopped in the staff locker room to hang up her coat and lock up her purse and keys. With an hour to spare before the start of her shift, she went straight to Joy's room.

Halting abruptly in the doorway when she saw a strange woman sitting in the rocking chair, holding Joy.

The woman's gaze was riveted on the baby, staring down at her with an expression of utter rapture. The woman hadn't glanced up when Krista entered the room.

Good heavens. The woman had to be Joy's mother.

CHAPTER FOURTEEN

KRISTA wasn't sure what to do—staying seemed an invasion of privacy but she found she simply couldn't leave, not without at least talking to Joy's mother. She set the bag of gifts on the floor near the doorway. As if her feet had a will of their own, they carried her further into the room.

The woman cradled Joy in her arms and the enraptured expression on her face eased the concern tightening Krista's stomach. Before she could introduce herself, Adam came into the room.

"Krista, I've been looking for you," he started, but then stopped when he caught sight of Joy's mother holding the baby. "Nancy?" He approached the woman. "Are you Nancy Williamson?"

The woman froze, staring at them with a wide, frightened gaze. She darted glances between both Krista and Adam, as if trying to figure out what they wanted from her.

"Are you Nancy Williamson?" Adam asked again.

Slowly the woman nodded.

"So you're Joy's mother? You left her in my clinic, but now you've come back to claim her?" Adam persisted.

A shadow of uncertainty darkened the woman's gaze. Krista could tell she didn't understand what Adam had said.

And suddenly the puzzle pieces slipped into place. She actually should have realized sooner. Stepping forward, she mouthed the word "mother" and used her right hand to spell out the word in sign language.

Nancy looked relieved and nodded again. She raised a hand and made several sign language gestures Krista didn't understand.

"I don't believe it," Adam said, glancing at Krista in amazement. "Joy's mother is deaf, too? How did you figure it out?"

Krista lifted a shoulder. "I could tell she didn't understand you. I think you spoke way too fast for her to read your lips." She turned back to Nancy, realizing just how this new news clarified things. "It makes sense now why she felt she couldn't take care of a baby all alone," she murmured. "I'm sure it's been very difficult, trying to raise a child when you can't even hear the baby crying. Did she have help? Or was she taking care of Joy all by herself?"

"I don't know." Adam blew out a breath. "We need to get Shirley in here as soon as possible."

"I agree." Krista didn't leave, though, but instead moved closer to Nancy and Joy. Using the only sign language she knew, the alphabet, Krista asked Nancy if she knew her baby was also deaf.

The shocked expression on Nancy's face confirmed Adam had been right—she hadn't known. Obviously, it had not occurred to Nancy to have Joy tested, maybe because the baby was so young. Nancy slowly shook her head, momentarily closed her eyes, holding Joy close.

"She didn't know about Joy's deafness," Adam said in a low tone. "No wonder she didn't turn around when I spoke to her that first day."

"You spoke to her?" Krista said in surprise.

"I saw her outside my clinic and suspected she was Joy's mother. When I called out to her, though, she ignored me, hurrying away."

Nancy stood up and carefully set Joy down in the crib. Then she pulled a small notebook and a stubby pencil out of her pocket and began to write. Krista exchanged a glance with Adam as they waited for her to finish.

She ripped the page out of her notebook and handed it to Adam. He read it out loud. "'Being a deaf woman raising a child who could hear seemed unfair. I couldn't talk to my child and sometimes I would see her crying and wondered how long she'd been upset. I didn't know how I was going to cope. I missed a few house payments and the bank threatened to foreclose on my loan. I loved Joy but I was scared. I wanted a better life for her than she'd have with me.'"

Krista blinked back tears.

Adam turned the note over and wrote back. Krista stepped closer to read over his shoulder. "I'll help you. There are plenty of resources available to you. There are ways to help you learn to care for a baby, systems that can be used to alert you to her crying. You're not alone in this."

Nancy took the note and her expression turned hopeful when she read what Adam had written. Then she wrote again, ripping the note off and handing it to Adam. "Am I too late? Does Joy belong to someone else?"

"No," Krista said, shaking her head. "You're not too late." She spoke slowly, emphasizing each word. Then she used sign language to spell the word "yours". She crossed over and picked Joy up, placing the baby back into Nancy's arms, demonstrating what she meant. "Yours," she repeated. "Joy is yours."

Nancy's eyes filled with gratitude. "Thank you," she mouthed. She lifted her fingers to her lips and drew them away, making the sign for thank you.

"You're welcome," Krista said in a low tone, realizing she wouldn't see Joy again but could rest easy, knowing the baby would be well cared for with a mother who loved her very much.

She couldn't ask for anything more.

Adam had wanted to have a few moments alone with Krista, but Nancy's arrival had caused a flurry of activity. There were forms to fill out, arrangements to be made before he could legally discharge Joy into Nancy's care. He was willing to make her payments himself to help get her back on her feet financially. Seeing as it was Christmas Eve, he couldn't imagine a better Christmas gift than reuniting a woman and her daughter.

Krista disappeared shortly after Shirley arrived, saying something about needing to get to work. At first he was worried she was upset, but when she gave Nancy a hug, he realized she wasn't upset at all. She'd claimed she wanted the best for Joy and she'd meant it. As usual, Krista was being her normal, generous self.

He knew he'd messed up, badly. Last night, after leaving Alec and Jillian at the hospital, he'd gone back to Children's Memorial, only to discover Krista had traded shifts, working the day shift to cover a sick call. He'd wrongly assumed she'd left work to see him at Trinity Medical Center.

Over and over again he wished he could go back and do things differently. To tell her first, before blurting out the news where she'd overheard. To explain why he'd kept the secret in the first place.

He'd tried her apartment, but she wasn't there either. The windows were dark and there was no sign of her car in the parking lot, so it didn't take a genius to figure out she wasn't home.

He'd tried calling, but she'd had her answering-machine on. He hadn't bothered leaving a message.

Better that he apologize in person.

It took him several hours to get everything arranged for Joy and Nancy. He talked the situation over with Shirley and agreed to keep Joy in the hospital until the day after Christmas. Nancy could spend the nights in Joy's room with her until then.

If only it was as easy to fix things with Krista. She had to work until eleven-thirty, giving him little choice but to wait for her to get off before they could talk.

He spent some time at his parents' house, helping to get food ready for the Monroe family celebration. He'd asked his family to hold off their gathering until early on Christmas Day, knowing Krista would be off work in the morning and would be able to attend.

If he could convince her to give him another chance.

He finished his Christmas shopping, spending hours picking out the proper gift for Krista. By eleven o'clock he couldn't stand waiting another minute. Even though he knew Krista still had a half-hour left on her shift, he drove over to Children's Memorial, his Christmas gift to her wrapped and sitting on the seat beside him.

Tucking the small wrapped box in his pocket, he made his way up to the sixth floor. When he saw Krista walking off the unit with a small group of nurses he realized he'd almost missed her.

"Krista? Do you have a minute?"

She didn't appear overly pleased to see him but paused and slowly nodded. "Sure."

He waited until the rest of the nurses had left them alone. Taking her arm in his hand, he steered her towards the small waiting area outside the unit, which happened to be empty. The Christmas tree in the corner gave the room a festive look.

How should he start? He took a deep breath and let it out slowly. "I'm sorry, Krista. You shouldn't have found out the way you did. I should have told you myself."

She didn't seem angry as she regarded him thoughtfully. "Why didn't you?"

He was silent for a long moment. He could give her lots of reasons, but there was only one that really mattered. "Because it was my fault."

"Your fault?" She frowned. "Danielle's miscarriage was your fault?"

"Yes. I was arguing with her that night, loudly. I didn't see the truck heading straight toward us until it was too late."

"Oh, Adam." She reached for his hand. He fought the urge to pull her closer, to lose himself in her embrace, to bury his face in her hair. "Danielle told me the accident was caused by a truck running a red light. It wasn't your fault."

"It was my fault." He stared down at their clasped hands. "There was time to avoid the accident. I tried, but it was too late."

After a long moment she said, "I don't agree. Would it have been your fault if you were laughing over some silly joke, instead of arguing?"

Her question caught him off guard. If he and Danielle had been laughing, having fun before the crash, would he still be plagued by guilt? "I don't know."

"I don't blame you for your son's death, Adam." Krista's smile was sad. "I only wish you could find a way to forgive yourself."

"I'm trying," he admitted. "Because of you."

She blinked. "Me?"

"Yeah. Losing Abe was bad enough, but losing you, Krista, would be much worse. When you left me at the hospital that night, I nearly went crazy, looking for you." He pulled the small wrapped box out of his pocket and handed it to her. "Will you, please, open this?"

She hesitated so long he thought she was going to refuse, but then she took the box and unwrapped it. Her eyes widened when she saw the jeweler's box, and she flipped the lid open, her gaze full of trepidation.

She silently stared at the ring. What was wrong? Did she hate diamonds? Damn, he should have asked, rather than assuming. He'd heard women often preferred to pick out their own engagement ring.

"If you don't like it, we can exchange it for something else." His words sounded stiff to his own ears.

"I don't understand, Adam." Her gaze held confusion. "Why are you giving this to me?"

What was not to understand? He frowned. "Because I love you."

"You do?" Her tone held a mixture of hope and disbelief. "I wish I could believe you, Adam. But every time you're hurt or upset, you close yourself off from me. I have to be honest—that behavior isn't exactly the foundation of a loving relationship."

He swallowed hard, panic threatening to choke him. "I know I've held myself back from you, Krista, and I'm sorry. I know I can't prove it, but I was going to talk to you the day I found out about Alec and Jillian. I've had so many regrets but turning around to see you standing there with that devastated expression on your face was the worst." He tightened his grip on her hand. "I'm sorry I hurt you. You're a beautiful, kind, generous person. Will you, please, give me another chance to prove how much I love you?"

He held his breath when she hesitated. After a few long, drawn-out moments she nodded. "Yes, Adam. Because I love you, too." He couldn't hide his elation, even when she held up a hand and added, "But I want you to share everything with me. I want you to tell me what you're thinking and feeling, even if you're afraid it might upset me."

It sounded easy, but he knew it wasn't. His elation faded and his gaze was serious, holding hers. "I'll try, Krista. I swear to you, I'll try." And he would, but hiding his emotions deep inside had become an ingrained habit, especially over this past year. He needed to be honest with her. "But old habits can be hard to break. It won't be easy, and you need to know I might slip up on occasion."

For the first time in days she smiled. "Well, at least you're being honest. I know you've hidden your emotions for a long time. I don't expect perfection, I just need to know you care."

"I do care, more than I can ever say." He reached out and drew her close. "I love you, Krista. I can't imagine my life without you."

"Oh, Adam," she murmured, throwing her arms around his neck and holding him tight. "I love you, too. I think I've always loved you since the night you came to rescue me." She pulled away, gazing up at him from eyes bright with tears. "I just didn't want to settle for being second best. Or for anything less than having your love."

"You could never be second best." He gently took the box from her hand, opened it and took out the diamond engagement ring. "And you will always have my love. Will you wear my ring?"

"Yes."

He slipped the ring on her finger with a sense of relief. "Thank heavens. My mother was ready to disown me for hurting you. And I was afraid Austin was going to ask you to marry him, just to make me mad."

That made her laugh. "He wouldn't do that."

"Yes, he would, because he knows a good thing when he sees it." He raised a brow. "I hope you realize exactly what you're getting into now that you've agreed to become a part of the Monroe family. My parents expect lots of grandchildren. I think I'd like to oblige them."

"I'm not worried." She smiled. "I'm going to love being a part of your family." She stood on tiptoe to kiss him.

He met her halfway, kissing her with a need born of desperation. Only the knowledge that they were still standing in the waiting room at Children's Memorial held him in check. He broke away while he still could.

"Merry Christmas, Adam." A hint of remorse shadowed her eyes. "I don't have a present for you."

"You've already given me a present, by forgiving me and agreeing to marry me. I love you, Krista." He drew her toward the elevator, knowing he was by far the luckiest Monroe in the clan. "Thanks to you, Christmas has just become my favorite holiday."

EPILOGUE

KRISTA watched as Adam's family surrounded Nancy and Joy Williamson, cooing over the baby and drawing them further into the kitchen, generally making them feel welcome at their Christmas family gathering.

She was so happy they'd agreed to come.

Nancy smiled and handed Joy over to Krista so she could take off her coat and scarf.

For a long moment Krista gazed into Joy's tiny face, until Nancy came back for her. She gave Joy back to her mother, pleased to see how Joy seemed to be enjoying all the attention.

"Having regrets?" Adam murmured near her ear.

"Not a single one." She'd been approved as a temporary receiving home caregiver and she'd been thrilled when Adam had agreed to be a part of the process, too. He liked the idea of helping kids in need as much as she did. "It was nice of you to invite them."

"The least I could do, considering Joy helped bring us together." Adam's smile warmed her all the way down to her frozen toes.

"Yes." The baby would always hold a special place

in her heart for that same reason. Joy was truly a miracle baby.

"What can I get you to drink?" Abe asked, holding up a dark bottle. "Spiced rum, anyone?"

He gave a cup to Nancy, who tentatively tasted the rum before grinning and holding up the cup for more. Everyone was speaking slowly and distinctly to Nancy to help ensure she could understand them.

And if not, Nancy always had her notepad handy.

Alec and Jillian seemed to be doing better, despite their recent loss. Jillian smiled and took Joy's tiny hand, her eyes barely revealing a hint of longing. Shelby didn't venture far from Jillian's side and she suspected that Alec and Jillian had put the miscarriage into perspective, knowing they already had a beautiful daughter to care for.

As the Monroe family gathered in the living room, near the giant, brightly decorated tree, Krista couldn't imagine being any happier than she was right at that moment.

"Can I have your attention?" Adam asked, his deep voice remarkably similar to his father's.

The group quieted down, looking up at him expectantly.

Adam drew Krista close to his side. "I'd like to announce our engagement. Krista has agreed to marry me."

"I knew it!" Abby shouted, jumping to her feet. "Welcome to the family, Krista."

She found herself being hugged and kissed by several members of the Monroe family. Even Austin had the audacity to kiss her directly on the mouth, sending her a secret wink when Adam frowned.

Nancy must have understood because she was

smiling and made a sign that Krista figured meant congratulations. Krista decided she really needed to brush up on her sign language.

"Good choice, Adam," Abe said, clapping his son on the back. "This time your mother and I wholeheartedly approve."

This time? She glanced at Adam, her brow raised questioningly.

"I'm glad, Dad." Adam grinned and pulled her close for a quick, hard kiss. "Because I think Krista is perfect for me, too."

Tears threatened and she blinked them back with an effort.

So this was how it felt to be part of a loving family.

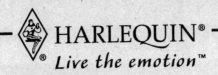

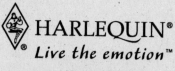

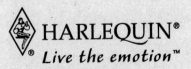

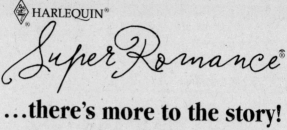
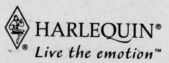

Harlequin® Historical
Historical Romantic Adventure!

*Imagine a time of chivalrous
knights and unconventional ladies,
roguish rakes and impetuous
heiresses, rugged cowboys
and spirited frontierswomen—
these rich and vivid tales will
capture your imagination!*

*Harlequin Historical . . .
they're too good to miss!*

SPECIAL EDITION™

Emotional, compelling stories that capture the intensity of living, loving and creating a family in today's world.

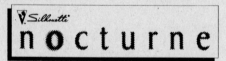

Modern, passionate reads that are powerful and provocative.

Dramatic and sensual tales of paranormal romance.

Romantic SUSPENSE

Romances that are sparked by danger and fueled by passion.